Yama ⌐

Text copyright © David Scurlock 2020

First published in the United Kingdom in 2024 by Yama
Publishing, Scotland Place Ramsbottom BL0 9 BD

A CIP record for this book is available from the British
Library.

ISBN 978-1-7384697-0-3

David Scurlock

THE MISSING SAMURAI SWORD

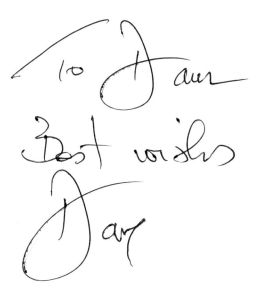

To Jаur

Best wishes

Jay

Chapter 1 The Headache

Jesus! My head hurts. What the hell hit me?

Why did I let Maisy talk me into trying to help her sister, Maggie, sort out her problems with her pimp? It had been nigh on impossible to find her house in the foul, sulphuric fog that blacked out the derelict backstreet. Looking up through the swirling fog, solitary chimneys appeared, standing there as if in memory of someone's home. The backstreet stank and rank smells reminded you of things you'd rather not remember. After falling over a bicycle and hitting the frost-covered cobbles headfirst,. I looked up to see a back door; it had the number painted on it I was looking for. I knocked. After a minute or two, I heard a key rasping in a lock, then some muffled footsteps. The door groaned as it scraped on the stone floor. Maggie appeared out of the gloom, nodded, turned on her heel, and I followed her into her two-up-and-two-down terrace. The door closed behind us. She switched on the lights, just a bare bulb that emitted enough light to see that the house was still in one piece.

The house had seen much better days. Now it had cold, damp walls, blotched and yellowed with mildew near the ceiling. A clean, grey oilskin covered the floor. A whiff of disinfectant hung in the air. Empty kitchen shelves added to the whole threadbare look of poverty. The only warmth filtered through the dank atmosphere from a fireplace filled with nutty slack. A plate with the remains of baked beans and Stork margarine were the only signs of habitation. Maggie sat at the kitchen table, a roll-up in one hand and a glass of gin in the other. She pointed to the only other chair. I sat down and looked her over: dyed, brassy, blonde hair with dark roots showing: a pinched, drawn face; a small nose; dark eyebrows, and a small tattoo under her left ear. She wore a little makeup, which failed to hide the bruises. Her lank frame suggested an underdeveloped teenager, and the off-pink dressing gown around her slender shoulders had seen better days. Staring at me through bloodshot eyes, she looked as rough as old boots.

"I told Maisy I could handle it myself. She always gets things arse about face."

By handling it, she meant to stop her pimp beating her up and stealing her money and her life.

"Maisy is worried about you. She just asked me to call around and see that you're alright."

"Please leave. It's really not good for you to be here."

I raised my eyebrows in a silent question, but she just took another drag on her cigarette, swilled some gin, and got up.

"I'll show you out through the front door; just turn left and keep going up towards the main road."

I sighed. This wasn't the time nor the place for a heart-to-heart.

"Okay, Maisy knows how to get in touch with me if you want to talk."

She looked me in the eye, a half smile on her lips, before she let me out of the front door and shut it after me. The air outside was hanging about like a foul blanket, the glow from the gas streetlight a mere candle in the gloom. As I started back up the street, I thought I heard a swish before something hit me on the back of the head. I almost passed out, but the shock of hitting the frozen pavement kept me conscious. I tried to get to my feet, but my legs wouldn't respond, and someone played a tune on my ribs. Thank God, the idiots weren't wearing winkle-pickers. My brain told me to get away. Instinct saved me or my training, I relaxed into survival mode and rolled along the curb away from the front door as fast as I could.

I heard voices. "Where is the bastard?"

"I can't see nothing," came a reply.

"Find him; hurt him."

On hands and knees, I inched along until my forehead touched the brick wall. I stood up and tried to melt my body into the brickwork. I stayed still and assessed the damage the idiots had dished out. Nothing felt broken. I edged my way up the street; their cursing soon became muffled, another sound lost in the murk. Now I was out of danger. I was getting mad, but it could wait; they could wait, and their time would come. I stayed glued to the walls, well away from the dull gleam of the gaslights, until I reached the corner of the street. I calmed down, gathered my bearings as best as I could, and kept close to the curb, picking my way along each street for what seemed an eternity, until, more by luck than judgement, I stumbled upon the main road. The road had better lighting, and before I knew it, I was standing outside "The Grapes," a place you could get a drink anytime if they knew you.

Chapter 2 A Bolt Hole

I shook the frost off my overcoat, knocked on the back door, and the peephole slid back.

"It's Eneko," I mumbled.

The door opened, and Morris, a Nigerian ex-middleweight journeyman fighter, nodded. He'd been around for years, and from what I'd heard, he'd never had to prove how tough he looked. I went past him and clung to the wooden bannister as I walked down the bare stone steps to the cellar. In the corner, a fireplace was glowing cherry red, with the crackling sound of burning coal creating its own brand of music. Light from the fire was throwing shadows on the walls. An electric light shone from behind the bar, so you could see the shelves of spirits. Red brick walls, a stone floor, and tables made of solid oak only added to the atmosphere. The air was heavy with tobacco smoke; an old tar in the corner was smoking his plug, its heady aroma pervading everywhere, but it still smelled better than outside.

The usual crew was in, with a couple of pimps at one end of the bar, one with a pock-marked face. They saw me and looked away. At the table by the wall, two big, florid-faced blokes in long overcoats were trying to disguise the fact that they were the law, but those big, black boots were a dead giveaway. In the back, against the wall, sat three ladies of the night huddled together around a table, no doubt discussing the finer facets of the male perspective. Here, everyone was off-duty, just seeking solace away from the madness and the din of the daily grind.

Albert, the owner, came over. He was an overweight, barrel-chested geezer with a bulbous beak of a nose that had broken veins, the telltale sign of a heavy drinker "The usual Eneko?"

I nodded. "But make it two large ones."

"Rough night?"

"I've had better."

Albert also owned the pub upstairs, but he rarely ventured into it. His daughter ran it. This cellar was his oasis for the insomniacs of the city. During the war, they had used it as an air raid shelter, and it still had that feeling about it. Somewhere safe and warm from the nightmares of the outside world. Albert had never got out of the habit; it suited him and like-minded souls.

He deposited the drinks, and I tried to gather my thoughts. Jesus! My head hurts. What a cock up, some bloody private detective! Albert delivered another drink and nodded. I sat in the warmth and safety, drinking and trying to get the fog out of my head. I must have dozed off because Albert shook me awake. "Eneko, it's 7 am"

Muttering thanks, I roused myself, paid Albert, and hauled myself up the stairs. Morris opened the door, nodded, and closed it behind me. Taking a deep breath proved it to be more unpleasant outside. I put one foot in front of the other; it hurt. Those kicks to the ribs weren't helping. I headed back to the office like a homing pigeon with a broken wing. It took a while; the fog was not getting any better. George had opened up the office and had the coffee on the go when I levered my aching carcass through the door.

George raised her eyebrows at me. "You look like the lady put up a fight," she intoned in her wonderful Welsh lilt, with a look of amusement on her lips. My eyes settled on the coffee. George poured me a cup, strong and black. Opening a packet of Passing Cloud, she lit one for herself and one for me. We smoked and drank in silence.

"Eneko, you look like a mess. You've got blood congealed down your neck and your cheek, for Christ's sake. Come over here." I shifted over to her office chair. She sat me down and started opening the desk drawers before coming up with some Dettol and a cloth.

"Bend your head forward," I did, and she went about cleaning my wound. My head was resting on her breasts. I felt at peace with the world. If I could just go to sleep, George smelled of earthiness and warmth.

"That'll have to do for now. Do you feel woozy?"

"I just need to rest here for about an hour."

George laughed and helped me up. She was 5 feet 10 inches with thick, black hair cut like Audrey Hepburn, flashing hazel eyes, long eyelashes, a straight, slim nose with a few freckles, and a small scar below her left ear. She had a beautiful glow to her healthy complexion and good, strong, white teeth. Broad shoulders that tapered to a slim waist and legs that went on and on.

"Eneko, are you ready for your interview with Senor Bengoa at 9:30 am?"

I mumbled, "Yeah."

"You don't look it, and you smell like something else. I suggest a shave and a long, hot shower. And put on your best clobber. That new blue suit I helped pick out for you last week is perfect."

I finished my coffee, stubbed my cigarette, and dragged myself to my apartment door. In the bathroom, I checked the back of my head. I found a lump, but nothing showed. I took a long, hot shower, shaved, and took stock of myself in the bathroom mirror. Not too shabby, I thought to myself. I made myself presentable in my new navy blue suit, clean pale blue shirt, navy blue socks, and black shoes. As I emerged from the apartment, a loud wolf whistle echoed across the room. I bowed. That was a mistake. The room swayed.

"You'll need your overcoat; it's Baltic out there, and a hat or your head will fall off before you make it to the appointment."

She stood in front of me and looked me in the eye; we were the same height and same age; she loved music, movies, Passing Cloud cigarettes, Rémy Martin, and so did I. That's where the similarity ended, or maybe it didn't. I adored women, and so did she.

"Better make an impression, Eneko. We need the money, or I do," she said.

I smiled and almost bowed again. George winced for me and helped me on with my beige Burberry Trench coat and matching trilby.

"Go get 'em, cowboy," she said as I headed out into the unrelenting, sulphurous soup we called fresh air.

The Fruit exchange appeared to be lively, with merchants still buying and bidding on produce and trucks all over the place. How the hell could they see what they were doing in that murk? I did not know. I crossed Victoria Street and headed up Temple Lane. They've started brewing early today, I thought, as the sweet, cloying smell of hops tried to ease the carbon mixture that was clawing its way into my lungs. Liverpool's finest sandstone buildings bore the result of many decades of coal smoke and exhaust fumes. I hoped my lungs weren't quite that bad. I walked up towards Dale Street, trying hard not to slip on the frosty cobbles in my new shoes. Pedestrians strode by, some wearing their scarves covering their noses like bandits in an old black-and-white cowboy movie. Dale Street was busy. Trams were clanking by and squeaking as they slowed for the slope on Water Street. Taxis were out in force, heading for the Pier Head and looking for custom. I walked up to the newsagents, its outer walls, resplendent with St. Bruno, Craven A, and Woodbine tin advertising hoardings. The door rang as I entered. Alf looked up and said, "Morning, Eneko, the usual?"

"Please, Alf." He put two packets of Passing Cloud on the counter. Black ink stained his hands, an occupational hazard from folding the morning papers. I paid and stuck the packs in my overcoat pocket.

Chapter 3 The Interview

My interview was with a client of Pedro Bengoa. Sr Bengoa was CEO of a Spanish/British shipping company. We met at a dinner at the Anglo-Spanish club here in Liverpool. Pedro Bengoa was, what we call, a gent. He was a proud Basque from a village near Bilbao. Quite tall with broad shoulders, black hair going grey at the sides, a large straight nose, a square jaw, and a ready smile. He walked like a man who had spent a lot of time at sea. I liked him. He loved football and was a proud season ticket holder at Anfield. It amused me that when he became immersed in the match, he developed a scouse accent.

At the dinner, he thought I was English until they introduced us. It delighted him when our host told him I spoke his native language, Basque. And that I had spent time in Spain during the Civil War as a war correspondent. We used to meet occasionally at the Anglo-Spanish Club. The conversation would usually start with football, then Basque life, and, of course, ships. He had never met my parents, but he knew some ships my father had worked on. Pedro Bengoa knew ships; he had an almost encyclopaedic knowledge of them, from fabrication to launching. Now in the throes of life after the war, his company office in Liverpool was desperately trying to get more involved with the booming Oriental economy, particularly Hong Kong and Japan. So when I mentioned that my mother was Japanese and I spoke the language, he'd hired me on the spot to assist him with his growing number of Japanese customers.

I arrived on time, and his secretary, Joyce, a very efficient-looking Scottish woman in a dark grey suit and black shoes, showed me into his office.

"Morning, Eneko."

His office was enormous, with high ceilings and large stained glass windows embossed with the company name. The fire in the hearth was blazing with olive logs, releasing their pleasant aroma. It had a centrepiece, an exquisite rosewood desk, resting on teak floors. Oak panelling covered the walls, from which hung large oil paintings of the company's ships through the last couple of centuries.

"May I introduce you to Senorita Alicia Begonia de Vera Cruz?"

I bowed Spanish style and said, "I hope you are having a pleasant stay in Liverpool."

She smiled. Her lips and eyes crinkled simultaneously. A mountain of luxurious hair cascaded down her back. Around her neck hung a gold crucifix, which stressed its length. Her lips were large, and her teeth looked strong and very white. A black business suit with a calf-length skirt and black flat shoes—she was too tall for heels—completed the outfit. Senorita Alicia Begonia de Vera Cruz was sensational, and she knew it.

She addressed me in Basque; I replied, and she smiled again.

Sr Bengoa laughed, "As we're in England, can we carry on this conversation in English, please?"

She laughed as well. "Please call me Begonia," she said. I could only detect a slight Home Counties accent.

Sr Bengoa clapped his hands. "Coffee," he said.

He pressed a buzzer, and Joyce appeared with a tray of cups and saucers, a large coffee pot, and some pastries. Joyce served them up and departed as swiftly as she entered.

"Eneko, Begonia has come to me with an intriguing proposition, one that I'm sure will interest you. Begonia used to work in Hong Kong and Japan. You can catch up later."

Sr Bengoa nodded to Begonia, who set out her proposition.

"A prominent family in Japan has asked me to find an heirloom that went missing at the end of the war and which is believed to be here in England."

"Do you know whereabouts in the UK?"

She shook her head and continued, "During the war, at the very end, really, a Japanese officer had his sword confiscated. The sword is a samurai sword made by Go Yoshihiro, a famous swordsmith from the 14th Century. I imagine the sword is worth a great deal of money, but it is a treasured family heirloom. Sr Bengoa has assured me of your reputation as a very thorough private investigator and one with impeccable credentials."

I smiled at Sr Bengoa and said, "That's very good of you. I hope I can live up to that introduction."

Begonia gave me a long, serious look. "I have left all the details with Sr Bengoa. Please read them, and if you wish to take on the case, I will send the funds to your office."

We exchanged business cards, and I said I would contact her in a day or so. She smiled again, and with that, she was gone.

I looked at Pedro, who raised his eyebrows. "Interesting," he murmured.

"She's a real Basque?"

Pedro nodded. "I know of her father."

I looked at him and asked, "Why me?"

"Who else, he replied." He pointed to an envelope on his desk. "All the information is there. I haven't read it. I understand nothing about Japan or Japanese artefacts, as you well know."

We shook hands. Pedro said he'd got tickets for the next home match if I fancied it.

I said I'd be in touch.

Chapter 4 George

As I stepped back out into the street, the omnipresent smog still cloaked the thoroughfare, and I could feel the damp sea air moving up Water Street from the Mersey—something else to add to another dank day. I needed to think. My head was still aching. I called George from a phone box and told her I was going to the Kardomah for coffee after picking up a cashmere scarf from Watson and Prickard.

"The interview?" she said.

"Tell you later," and put the phone down.

I sauntered along to the shop. I had a quick chat with Lavina, who was my fashion guru, always keeping me abreast of any new fashion trends that I should know about. She said my trench coat looked wonderful and my scarf would go well with my new suit.

She asked after George, "Can you tell her the underwear she ordered has arrived?" And gave me a knowing grin.

I smiled, left, and made my way to Church Street, taking care of the frosty cobbles. Trams and buses appeared almost before you could see them, keeping the office wallahs on their tiptoes. I kept going until I could see the glow and smell the aroma of fresh coffee emanating from the Kardomah. There were only a few customers, which was fine with me. Ruby, my favourite waitress, came over with my coffee. She had a classic blonde beehive with a fringe, bright red, ruby lipstick, and a scouse accent you could cut with a knife. I loved it. With a hearty "All right, En," she plopped the coffee on the table and left me to it. Scousers shortened everything, even short names. I remembered at school that one of my friends was Emile Pierre Andre Marouse and was called Milo, naturally. I lit another cigarette just as Ruby arrived with my second coffee. "Is George alright, En? I haven't seen her for a while. You must be working that poor girl too hard," she said with a twinkle in her eye.

George! I depended on that young Welsh lady, George, who began working for me by complete chance: Late one spring night, I was walking back to my place, and as I cut through Mathew Street, I heard raised voices, two louts effing and blinding, beating up someone who was taking a right hammering. As I approached them, the one on the receiving end hit the deck hard, and as the body smacked the cobbles, I saw she was a girl. I didn't wait for introductions. I just hit the first lowlife in the ribs and followed that with a chopping punch to the side of his neck, and he collapsed to the ground with a groan. His mate brought out a knife. He looked like he'd used one before. He circled me, feinting left and right before launching an attack on my midriff. I blocked it and delivered two punches to the ribs and a knee to the stomach, followed by a roundhouse kick to his head.

The girl looked a mess, with blood running from her nose. She was pretty much incoherent, and her legs were incapable of mobility, so I half carried her back to my office and sat her down on the couch. Her face was bruised and blood caked on her face: and one eye looked a mess— the makings of a real shiner! A quick examination showed no knife wounds to her body, but more bruising. She was still woozy, and I could smell brandy on her breath. I bathed her face with warm water and got rid of the blood. Her clothes were in tatters; they reeked of sweat and cheap perfume, stained with god knows what from the cobbled street. I ran a bath; my tub was Japanese style—it took a while to fill.

She still hadn't moved. I looked her over, checking to see if she had any more bruises on her head. I couldn't find any. Her tattered blouse was hanging off her back. I took her blouse off; her bra came with it; I got rid of it; I removed her ripped skirt; and the remnants of her briefs fell to the floor. The bruises on her ribs were already turning black and blue, and she had scratches on her back and legs. Manhandling her to the bathroom and lowering her into the bath wasn't a task for someone not in shape. She didn't stir as I washed her hair. She looked up and smiled, but said nothing. I added some herbs to the water to help with the bruising and made sure she didn't slide down the bath. I let her soak for about 30 minutes. She showed signs of regaining consciousness, so I put my arms under her shoulders and pulled her out. That was hard work. She was a dead weight. I wrapped her in one of my dressing gowns and put her in my double bed. On the bedside table, I put two large, fluffy towels, a glass of water, and a packet of aspirin. I left the door to the bathroom open with the light on. An interesting way to end the evening! I had a brandy, called it a day, and slept on the couch in the office.

In the morning, I got up around 7 am; she hadn't stirred, so I caught up on some paperwork. Around 9 am, the phone started ringing, and the enquiries kept me busy for a while. The office door rang. The postie arrived with a load of stuff for me. As I began sorting it, I heard a movement in the apartment. She was up and about.

I put the coffee on and looked around for some food—nothing, only biscuits and Rémy Martin. She emerged, wrapped in a fluffy white dressing gown, showered but with no makeup and a lovely shiner.

I said, "Hi, how are you feeling?"

She looked at me and said, "Good morning. How the hell did I get here?"

I noted the Welsh twang and explained what had happened.

"My head hurts, as do my back, my ribs, and my arse."

"You'll be okay in a few days."

"Who are you?"

I told her my story. A private investigator just started out 18 months ago.

"Did you undress me last night?"

"Yes, you were incapable."

"Of what?"

"Anything. I hope you don't think I took advantage of you?"

"Not the way I smelled"

"May I ask what you're doing in Liverpool?"

"I'm looking for a job. This is only my third day here, staying at the YWCA."

I passed her a coffee and offered her a Rémy and a biscuit. She settled for a coffee.

"Are you still looking for a job?"

She nodded.

I said, "I'm looking for a man Friday." She raised an eyebrow. I said, "A girl Friday." She raised both eyebrows. I said, "A personal assistant." She smiled. I explained the duties and that she would be my first employee.

She said that she could type but was more used to outdoor work, with the animals on the hills at her parent's place in Wales, but she wanted a change.

"Why me?" she asked?

"You impressed me with the way you handled last night under difficult circumstances. You fought bravely against overwhelming odds and have recovered quickly. That takes sangfroid, a quality highly regarded in this business. And I've seen you naked, so you have to be my secretary. It's the law."

She half smiled, but the shiner made it look like an effort. She looked at me. "Did you like what you saw?"

"Absolutely."

"Salary?"

"£10 a week."

"That's a bloody fortune. Does that include providing full service for the boss?"

This time I looked her in the eyes and said, "£10 a week gets me a loyal, hard-working employee who always acts with discretion and holds everything we do here in confidence."

The phone started ringing again. I said, "Think it over, have some more coffee, and then we'll talk."

I answered the phone. "Sora speaking." Another inquiry; this was getting ridiculous.

The phone rang again. I stretched to reach it, but the receiver had gone, "Good morning, George speaking, Mr Sora's secretary. Can I take a message?"

That's how we met. I called Lavina and asked her to talk to my new assistant about some office wear and get it delivered this afternoon. George looked flabbergasted, so I left them to it. At the end of her first working day, still in her office attire, she was about to go off to the

YWCA. I said I didn't think that was a smart move, with her facial injuries and heavy bruising.

She gave me a look. "Are you suggesting I spend the night in the safety of your fond embrace?"

I laughed, "Follow me, ye of little faith."

My office is on the ground floor, with my living quarters behind it. The entire building was mine, inherited from my parents. Once it had been a warehouse for various imported goods, but more recently for storing and bottling Port and Sherry before they had left it vacant. On the first floor above my office were two small apartments and a large space that was unused. To reach the first floor, you had to go up a wrought iron staircase. I opened the first apartment door and walked in. The place was dusty but furnished; it had a fireplace and an old but serviceable sofa, two bedrooms, a kitchen, and a bathroom.

"I think you should stay here until you are back on your feet and the bruising has gone. And if you like the job, this is the hidden extra for providing the boss with a hard-working secretary. The place will need some work to make it more like home, but I'm sure you'll manage."

She looked shocked to the core. "Jesus, boss, I'm not worth it."

"Then prove yourself wrong. See you at 8 am."

Chapter 5 My Little Secret

What I didn't tell George was that the building had many hidden features: all the windows had Rejas, Spanish ornamental grilles, which made it very difficult to break in. And solid oak doors, 6 inches thick. The floors were all hardwood, ebony in my apartment, and mahogany in the two smaller ones. They constructed the exterior of the building in stone, and the interior walls were red brick. My apartment was enormous. It comprised a sumptuous lounge with a fireplace, an adequate dining room, a simple Japanese-style bedroom with a large double bed, and a lavish dressing room. The bathroom was also Japanese-styled, between the lounge and the bedroom.

The part of the apartment I loved was a concealed door at the side of the lounge, which led, via a passageway, to a wrought iron spiral staircase that took you to the cellar. This was the only entrance. Originally, there had been an entrance that opened out onto the road, but I had replaced it with a stone wall. The basement had stone flags because it housed a wine cellar. But I had built a photographic study, complete with a darkroom, a gym, and a drying room for washing. I'd kept one wine rack that reached the ceiling; fine vintages were ageing in oak barrels. Alongside the wine racks were a dozen barrels of brandy. The largest barrel was empty and had a secret door that led to another cellar that was completely hidden from prying eyes. This part of the cellar had been dug out many years ago and was not on any local plans. I kept my martial arts equipment and my collection of Kendo sticks, Samurai swords, and pistols here. I had a Beretta 1934 from my days in Spain, a Browning Hi-Power, and a Colt M911A1 from an American friend in Japan. I'd also installed a shooting gallery. 6 feet wide and 100 feet long.

Since George started working for me, my business has prospered. With George in the office, I had more time for personal contact with clients, which was a major bonus. Now the office ran like clockwork, the paperwork was in order, and George had an instant rapport with people. Her Welsh accent charmed them.

I looked at the heavy brown envelope that Pedro had given me, resting next to my coffee cup. It looked intimidating. I opened it and inspected the contents: a photo of the Samurai sword on a stand; another photo of a Japanese officer in military uniform holding it. No names, no pack drill. An accompanying letter echoed what Begonia had explained with a couple of added facts. They believed it left Japan on a White Star ship in the late 40s heading for

Liverpool and two names: Captain Owens and William Mansell.

That was a while ago! Time to investigate, but it also got me thinking.

Chapter 6 My Heritage

My father was born in Spain, a proud, broad-shouldered Basque with enormous arms and a very charming smile. Born in 1883, he spoke English, but with a thick Basque accent. His father was a shipyard worker, Abarran Arrigorriagakoa, who went to work in the shipyards in Bilbao in the 1880s. He married a local Basque girl, Arantxa Urberuaga, and they had my father, Xavier Abarran Arrigorriagakoa. My mother was born in Chile, the daughter of a Japanese immigrant, Hiroshi Endo, who married a local girl, Harumi Matsui, who was second-generation Japanese. At home, they spoke Japanese, so my mother was fluent in both languages, and at school, she studied English. My parents met in Valparaiso in 1911, where my father was working as a ship's engineer for a Bilbao-based engineering company. His work came to a juddering halt when World War I got into full swing, but he stayed and worked when he could. My mother's parents lived inland, in a small village, when an earthquake struck Valparaiso in 1914. The family home was obliterated, and her parents died, but my mother, who was an only child, survived. In late 1917, my father was transferred to work at Cammell Laird in Merseyside. It was a real wrench for my parents, but they took to the lifestyle like ducks to water and soon became immersed in the culture of the city. They loved the city and its people; they felt at home in a friendly city. The house rules were: mom spoke to me in Japanese and Spanish, dad in Spanish and Basque. Outside, I only ever spoke in English with my friends; my language skills were irrelevant.

As a young child, I had vague recollections of my mother making strange-looking clothes at home. I loved them because they were so colourful. They were Chilean ponchos, which were colourful and warm. My mom used to make them for all my girlfriends. They made me a hit with the girls. School was okay, as I enjoyed writing and languages. But being a bit of a loner, I was happier running and boxing. I had a head start at boxing because my mother had insisted on me learning Karate and Judo from a very young age. Leaving school at 16, I got a job at the Liverpool Echo, covering local stuff and sports. But I was impatient to write about something important. The Spanish Civil War had just begun, so I took a chance to make a name for myself as a war correspondent.

Mom and dad both thought I was much too young, and I know they worried about me. I imagined I could see them smile when I spent free time with their cousin Jesus, an ex-skipper.

He was a confirmed bachelor and lived in a beautiful village, Castropol, in Asturias. Jesus used to call me the chameleon, as he said I blended into any environment and, with my language skills, I'd make an excellent spy!

"Make sure you keep that under your beret," I laughed.

It turned out he was almost right. I got arrested covering a story in the battle for Belchite in '37. The ability to speak Spanish, Basque, and English got me into loads of scrapes as neither side could abide journalists. In a skirmish, my shoulder took a bullet. I would have died if a German lad, Hans, hadn't rescued me and pushed me into an ambulance! Back in Castropol, I recovered with the help of Uncle Jesus and got back to work within weeks. After a couple more lucky breaks, the civil war ended in April of '39. I'd had enough of Spain and the madness of brothers fighting brothers, so I took a break in Bayonne in France. There, sanity prevailed for a while. Then, with the bayonet rattling of summer '39, my parents implored me to stay with Jesus and keep out of trouble now war was imminent. I kicked my heels in Asturias, learning the art of fishing with Jesus on his boat and trying hard not to get involved in WW11. One morning I was having breakfast in the main square. Jesus saw me, and with tears in his eyes, he handed me a telegram. The Luftwaffe had killed my parents in an air raid on Liverpool two weeks ago.

Distraught and much too late for the funeral, I went back to work as a war correspondent. I covered the whole North African campaign and then the Allied invasion of Sicily and Italy. After Egypt, I suffered from flashbacks and depression brought on by a concussion. Too close to too many artillery explosions. In Italy, I began my recovery and kept out of the final push to Germany as I covered the desolation of Italy. But I was far from cured. I was a broken man: too much killing, human wreckage, and ruins everywhere. I went to visit Jesus in Spain and he suggested lots of sunshine, wine, women, and song. It sounded like a plan, but before long I'd had enough of Franco's Spain, so I left and returned to Liverpool. December 1945 came and all the celebrations were over when I arrived back in England.

After a couple of meetings with editors, it soon became crystal clear that war correspondents were a luxury they could no longer afford. It embarrassed them to have a young war correspondent on their hands with no way of making him productive. Taking stock, I wasn't that bothered. My journalistic career had run its race, I was tired. I looked around, trying to pick up the pieces of Liverpool life was bewildering. Time to see a doctor who knew something about war and its issues. He recommended a specialist on Rodney Street. He was sympathetic to a point. Stating the obvious, he said I was exhausted and living on my nerves.

I didn't mention my occasional panic attacks, which reduced me to a shaking wreck for a couple of hours. He suggested a long, relaxing holiday, if I could afford it! In Liverpool, the pain was ever present, so was the poverty. I felt sorry for myself and then guilty, as I was far better off than most. The city looked in a state of shock. The trams were still running and the "Dockers Umbrella" was still carrying its passengers above the dock road. Feeling at my wit's end, I took a long walk along the docks, where merchant ships were loading and unloading as if nothing had happened. Merchant sailors were around having a pint or two. Soon after ordering one myself, I struck up a conversation with an officer, who said they were heading for Hong Kong and then Japan.

"When are you sailing?"

"The day after tomorrow," he said.

"Do you take passengers?"

"Speak to the Captain over there."

The Captain looked at me. I could see him turning the idea over in his head.

"I hope you like looking out of portholes."

We shook hands on a price and he asked me to be there by 4 pm as they would sail on the evening tide. Two days later, I boarded one of the Barber Lines finest steamers heading for Hong Kong and all points East. Onboard, the voyage gave me time to think without worrying about fighting, deadlines and more tragedy. The ship's officers and men looked like good, tough professionals. No doubt they'd seen horrors themselves during the war, but they never mentioned it. I caught up on my reading, glimpsing the sea between pages and when I wanted company, I joined the card school.

The steamer sailed on, slicing through the waves with reverence. Only docking occasionally, but I wasn't interested. Japan, and only Japan, was what I had in my focus. I had hopes for that strange but captivating country. Since my teenage years, when I understood my background, I'd held a secret desire to visit the land of my grandmother. What I would do, I did not know. It just felt the right thing to do. Hong Kong was a mass of ships, shops, and bars, and people going about their living. The ship sailed and headed to Japan, past Formosa and southern Japan, finally docking in Yokohama. It felt much cooler than Hong Kong and the city looked a total mess. The port was struggling to recover from the war, but it acted like a working port with ships from all over the world. Sailors and dockers were all over the place. I sensed hope in the air.

My mind drifted back to the envelope. I was sure many Samurai swords had disappeared after the war. But this sword stuck out as a unique one, one that would carry prestige. I needed more coffee and another cigarette. Nothing was coming to mind, so I waved to Ruby and drifted off back to the office.

George was eating a sandwich and drinking coffee.

She looked up. "Well, do you like the new look?"

Wow! George had been going on about changing the look of the office for some time. Now on the wall above the office door were photos of ships my father had worked on; on the back wall was a bookcase full of my books on Liverpool, its docks, maps, and legal books. On the opposite wall, a detailed map of Liverpool and some glorious photos of the docks, trams, the Overhead railway, and the Mersey itself. George had put some effort into moving and planning the new office look!

"How the hell did you get the bookcase in?"

"I'm not just a pretty face, boss."

I went to kiss her on the cheek, "Hang on, look at my pièce de résistance."

Looking around, I couldn't see it. George sat down at her desk, rested her face on her hands, and looked at me. I looked at her and then I saw a small photo in a red leather frame of me, dad and the Liverpool goalkeeper, Elisha Scott. I looked about 7 or 8.

"Where did you find it? I thought I had lost it for good."

"I found it in a case under the bed in the second bedroom. Do you like it?"

"I bloody love it." I kissed her on both cheeks. "You're a star, George, you really are."

She looked as pleased as Punch. "Go on, what happened this morning?"

I explained my morning excursion and its ramifications.

She grimaced at me, "Wow, what a case."

I mumbled agreement, then a thought struck me, "George, find out if William Mansell is involved in shipping in Liverpool or the UK?"

"Okay Sleuth," she said: "Try one of the new partners of that tie up between Oriental Line and the North American Line. They are operating out of here with offices in Hong Kong, Tokyo, Singapore, Panama, and New York."

I gave her a quick look.

"It's all in the newspapers, Eneko. Oh, sorry I forgot, ex-newshounds don't read papers. The library usually has back copies."

"Okay Miss Holmes, go check it out at the library and bring me all the lurid details."

She curtsied, grabbed that awful green duffle coat she wore and left. I tried on my new scarf, looked good and felt terrific. It went rather well with my new suit.

Chapter 7 Begonia

I gave the office a miss for the rest of the afternoon and wandered up to Chinatown, whose lights glinted through the deepening gloom. In between buying some groceries, I waved to my old mate Geoffrey Chang, the owner of the shop, who looked snowed under. Some ideas were taking shape as I stepped out down Bold Street, and to add to the stubborn gloominess, the drizzle had now become a more slushy sleet. I put my head down and marched towards Central Station, trying not to lose an eye on some errant umbrella, and continued on through Cases Street and into Rushworths on Whitechapel. I had ordered The Great Artistry Of Django Reinhardt, which was released late last year. Almost impossible to get, but Mike, who worked there, had his sources—I figured he knew people out at the American Base at Burtonwood, but I said nothing. With my head full of ideas, I headed back to the office. George had gone but had left a typed essay of everything that was William Mansell and his business interests. Alongside it sat a vanilla envelope with my name written on it in a fine feminine hand, from Begonia, no doubt. I changed into something more casual: grey slacks, grey shirt, thin-red angora sweater, black moccasins and a dark-grey top coat.

The evening air was colder, the light sprinkling of sleet had become thicker, and the atmosphere was as opaque as ever. As I edged along the lane and found Mathew Street, a figure started to materialise and come into focus. A slim figure in a dark coat.

"Hi, handsome," the voice said in Basque.

I laughed and said, "How can you tell in this fog?"

She walked up to me, kissed me on the cheek and joined me as I walked into the warm glow of the White Star. The landlord, an ex-military police officer, ran a tight ship. No idiots allowed in and no kids. We sidled past the bar and went to the back room. It was empty. The room smelled of leather polish and Brasso. The hearth was full of coal, an inviting glow reflecting off the brass fixtures.

Sydney, the landlord, said, "Evening, Eneko"

I said, "Evening, Sydney quiet tonight?"

"They're all at home watching the bloody tele. That thing will be the death of the pub. You mark my words."

I nodded in agreement and ordered a pint and a gin and tonic. He produced a beer that fitted into the glass, not a drop wasted. Begonia and I went back to the corner of the fireplace. She looked at me, waiting for me to say something. She was a beauty. Her hair almost reached her waist and shone with vitality. Today, she had on black slacks and a red sweater topped with a black duffel coat.

She said, "Eneko, I need to confess something. I met Yua at a photographic exhibition in Tokyo. I know a lot about you from Yua. She's a big fan, you know. She told me about your martial arts studies and also that you studied Buddhism. She also said that you were a passionate man."

I smiled. "She told you about her sex life?"

"Yua and I were more than just friends." She smiled. "You don't look surprised?"

"I'm not. Why should I be?"

She smiled again. Intriguing! Why had a fellow Basque taken me into her confidence so soon after our first meeting?

"But now Eneko, you're here in Liverpool, I want to know why a fellow Basque likes Liverpool so much?"

"That's a question and a half! I'll tell you later in my apartment."

As we drank, I tried to explain about my job and why l enjoyed it. But it felt difficult to explain in the pub.

We left and, with Begonia clinging to my arm, we made it back to my place without mishap. I opened the office and walked through to my apartment.

She took a deep breath as she entered. "Wow, this is amazing."

She sat down on a leather couch and looked around, taking in my personal artefacts and taste in art. I made coffee and poured two large glasses of Rémy. She stood up and inspected the far wall. I had my favourite prints: Men on a Suspension Bridge; The Dream of a Fisherman's Wife; The Amida Waterfall. And next to that was a print by Pablo Picasso: Woman and Octopus. Below that lay some low tables with my collection of teapots and cups, and stoneware sake bottles and Bernard Leach's, A Potter's Book. The next table had my collection of Shunga prints by Utagawa Kunisada. On the near wall was a bookcase full of my favourite writers, in Basque, Spanish and some in Japanese. She also looked at my favourite book on yoga: Hatha Yoga by Theos Bernard. Begonia laughed when she saw my books by Lafcadio Hearn.

"Does George like these prints?"

"She just laughed when she saw them, but I saw her inspecting them. Another coffee and Rémy, Begonia?"

"Yes, please."

I noticed she had found another book of untitled prints. It contained modern woodblock prints of women in the bath house in various poses of washing, arranging and combing their hair. Begonia looked at them with interest. "These are gorgeous. Did Yua do them?"

I said, "Yes, Yua's very talented."

Begonia kept going through the prints. Yua had dedicated the last part of the book to Shunga. Begonia smiled, "I've never seen these prints, Yua's secret collection?"

The prints were of women in various states of undress cavorting with each other, and one of a naked girl on her knees getting spanked by a woman with a bamboo cane. Begonia laughed. "Yua's saucy side, I see. Oh, that's brilliant," she flipped back to the beginning of the book and pointed to a photo of Yua and family and some Buddhist monks working in the garden at her ryokan.

"I see the TV there. Have you ever watched it?"

"Not really. To be honest, I bought it last year to watch the Coronation. And George watches it. They say it's the coming thing."

"Now tell me about your life in Japan before becoming a private detective. "

"Begonia, I could bore you to death with my heart-rending tale of post-war drama."

"No, I'm interested. It sounds fascinating."

Chapter 8 My Time in Japan

"Okay, I worked as a war correspondent during the Civil War in Spain. My parents both died in the August 1940 air raids on Liverpool while I was in Spain. Then I covered the whole North African campaign, and the Allied Landing in Sicily and Italy. The final push to Germany got along fine without me. I covered the desolation and aftermath of WW11 in Italy.

When I rediscovered Liverpool, it looked like a shell of its former self, and so was I. Consumed by grief and guilt, with shattered nerves I felt guilt because I was alive, a witness to so much bloodshed, death, and suffering. Life, I felt, had passed me by. I struggled to sleep and when I did, my dreams were full of death and the dying. I imagined I could still smell the stench of war; it smells the same in any language. I knew I had to exorcise the demons, so on a whim I visited the land of my mother's family, Japan.

The ship docked in Yokohama, which, as you know, was battling to get back to some form of normality. I boarded a train to Tokyo, I couldn't believe my eyes, broken buildings, destroyed roads. The fire bombs had only left scorched remains; broken signs for a barber shop, telephone wires flapping in the breeze. The entire Tokyo area was a mess. It seemed like I'd come from a European bombsite to an Oriental one.

At Tokyo Station, I boarded a train heading west. The other passengers eyed me. Matching clothes and a leather suitcase drew attention in Tokyo, 1946. I kept my feelings in check and stayed seated until it reached its destination. Night had fallen, and I couldn't make things out. I enquired at the station about finding somewhere tranquil. The uniformed man at the ticket office looked at me, smiled and directed me to another train, telling me to get off at a place called Hachioji. I did as I was told. At my destination, a small hut served as a ticket office. I asked the ticket collector about finding somewhere to stay. He took his hat off and scratched his head, then he smiled and directed me to a small ryokan that was looking for customers.

After thanking him, I walked through the evening air, through bamboo groves to the ryokan, with only the sounds of the cicada for company. The air was clear, and the smells were not of anything I recognised. I walked with some kind of trepidation in the cool night air. I couldn't see where I was going, a glimmer now and again when the moon broke through the clouds helped me, so I kept going. A glow in the road moved towards me. It turned out to be an old man carrying a lantern. He stopped, and we spoke. He asked where I was going. I answered, and he pointed to another lantern that looked to be about two hundred yards away. I thanked him and, feeling more confident of my direction, strode out. The ryokan looked tidy. A lantern with the name, "Peaceful Life" on it hung at the entrance. I announced myself—the customary way of doing things in Japan and a kimono-clad woman came to the door and invited me in. After a couple of days of acclimatising, I soon got to know the place and started going for walks in and around Takao. I ventured up the mountain through the bamboo grooves one day and saw the temple near the top. According to my new friend at the ryokan, Yamabushi still practised their particular school of Buddhism there.

Yua Kawabata, the owner suggested that if I was going to stay for an extended period, I should rent the small guest house they had on the back of the property. It would be cheaper and offer more privacy and my meals and bathing could still be in the ryokan. Yua had two children, Reo, 9 and Sara, 7, and she was married to Hidefumi Kawabata, a soldier who they led her to believe was still in a Russian prisoner of war camp.

Yua was a striking woman of around 34. She was slim, with long hair, a very clear complexion and a wonderful laugh. She longed to know about the west and its culture. I told her I was an inadequate teacher, but she implored me to tell her what I knew. I even explained about my life as a war correspondent and the battles and the destruction left behind. And my fears and guilt about not taking part as a soldier and just being an observer. She listened and got me to write essays about Hachioji in English, then I'd translate to her and she would write them in Kanji, something I'd never mastered. But Yua taught me. I felt more relaxed and happier, less troubled. Yua said I needed to toughen up. She said she studied Kendo, an excellent discipline for physical and mental wellbeing. She would speak to the local monk and the Kendo teacher. So under her tutelage, I began studying Kendo, Aikido, and Karate. As well as Shingon Buddhism, to calm and control my mind.

I took classes as an outsider and began my physical training by running up Mount Takao through the bamboo groves. I loved it. Memories of my youth came flooding back. My physical stamina improved with each passing week. The climate in and around Takao has four definite seasons: winter was cold with snow, spring with cherry blossoms and the sounds of growth, summer was humid and sweaty, autumn was lovely with all the leaves changing colour and clean fresh air. I loved my time there and also living in my guest house.

Yua was a fascinating woman who wrote poetry and short stories for her children to take them to school. I earned my keep by teaching children at the local school English. They were bright and very cheeky. I felt at one with the world. In the evenings, I would come back from training with more than a bruise or two and Yua would have the bath ready. I'd bathe and then soak in the main bath. I'm sure I looked shocked when Yua joined me in the bath for the first time, although I knew men and women bathed together. When she had quests, I sometimes joined them and I'd hear the women talking to Yua and passing comments about my muscles. You can't hide anything in Japan.

"Did Yua hope her husband would come back in one piece?"

"As you know, Yua was a Zen Buddhist, and she had genuine faith, something I lacked. In the locality, there were women who made herbal medicines and remedies for various ailments which Yua was involved with, so I studied them too. She was also very keen on her woodblock artistry and Shunga in particular, she used to get local women to pose. They were always keen, as they were quite an unabashed group. They used to come into the bathhouse at the ryokan and Yua would make sketches, they'd laugh and mess around and give me the once over and make rude jokes.

One night after bathing, Yua asked me, "If I liked women. I replied, "Yes." She smiled and asked, "Why I hadn't taken up the many offers her girlfriends had thrown out." I didn't know what to say.

She laughed and said, "Around here, you are a cockerel loose in the farmyard."

"That made me laugh, so we became lovers, or I became her pupil in the art of pillow talk. And not long after, I lived the life of a cockerel with most of the local ladies.

As time passed, I continued with my studies and I noticed that my body had changed shape. My muscle definition stood out. Yua commented on my muscles and energy. I felt strong, healthy, and calm. I sensed I was coming to terms with my guilt and anger at not being a soldier in the war, and frustration at not being able to help my parents leave Liverpool. People commented on how well my martial arts studies were going. I felt like a local.

The ryokan needed some repairs. Yua was worried, so I paid for the repairs and became a 10% partner in the business. I also bought the plot of land next to the ryokan, some 5000 square metres for a vegetable and herb garden. Yua clapped her hands and didn't stop talking about growing this and that.

One day I got back from studying and I found her crying in floods of tears. Her husband was alive and was due home in 3 months. One evening after bathing, she looked me in the eye and said she now had to wait for her husband. I smiled and agreed, though with a heavy heart.

That Friday evening I was reading in my guesthouse when Yua called in to say that her friend, Yumi, would like to learn English.

The next day at breakfast, Yua smiled and said, "It sounded like an interesting lesson last night." After that, new students arrived every Friday.

Then, out of the blue, in the autumn of 1949, Yua's husband, Hidefumi, arrived back from Russia. Yua and the children were ecstatic, though a little nervous. Hidefumi was distant at first, not sure what was going on. He was thin, almost skeletal, and didn't have any energy to do much. But week after week, you could see the improvement. You could tell he was getting back to normal. He started playing with his kids— they ran him ragged. We began speaking about war and its effects. I told him my story of only being an observer, and he told me a bit about the fighting and lots about the prison camp in Siberia. One day, he fixed the floor on the veranda. Yua winked at me. He did a superb job. In a previous life, he had been a carpenter. Yua laughed when I spent time with Hide. Life went on and I became friends with Hide. Over the months, he put on some weight and got his appetite back. We shared a fondness for sake.

I continued with my martial arts studies and progressed well according to my teachers. Then one day, young Sara became ill with pneumonia. They gave her Penicillin, a new treatment, but Sara didn't improve. We took her to the hospital, where a doctor attending to her said that the penicillin she took was contaminated. Time stood still for Yua, Hidefumi, and Reo. Their friends and the priest from the local temple came to offer their help. I felt at a loss about how to help, but I knew one thing: I felt genuine anger for the first time in a long while. At the US base in Tachikawa, I begged the doctors for some penicillin, even offering my services as a translator. The doctor agreed and gave me some. I raced back to the hospital and gave the doctor the penicillin. Sara regained her health and Yua and Hide almost did cartwheels. I think Sara being ill and recovering gave Hide a real boost, and he seemed to gain confidence overnight. After years in Siberia, you develop inner strength in order to survive. He worked hard on the ryokan and developed the vegetable garden, so they would be self-sufficient. One afternoon, I came back from studying and he presented me with a pair of wooden geta, wooden sandals, which everyone wore. He had made them himself and, for the rest of the family, another string to his bow!

I continued helping the doctors on the base with translation work and loving my new role liaising with the medical team. Things got edgy when I helped investigate missing medical supplies. I was warned it could be dangerous, but I took to it like a duck to water—embracing it totally. I decided there and then that's what I wanted to do. Things got tricky when the Yakuza distributed methamphetamine and heroin.

Both sides in the war had used them to boost confidence and stamina in their troops, so now we had a glut. The Yakuza saw it as a business opportunity, big money, little risk and easy to get hold of from American and Allied sources. My investigations had led me to some big names on both ends of the chain. People you don't want to annoy. I trained with Police officers, when practising Kendo and Aikido. Some of them were involved with the proposed new riot police force. They trained hard and led a pretty spartan life. One night after training, one of them pulled me to one side and warned me that my name had come up when they were interrogating some local thugs."

"Not good, Eneko, be on your guard."

"About a week later, as I was walking back from the base, three local gangsters, the ones with the little finger missing and covered in tattoos, the Chimpira, attacked me. In their eyes I was just a translator, an itch that needed to be scratched, so they only sent three men. Two were just lightweights, and I dropped both of them with well-aimed kicks that surprised them. The third was older, with stone dead eyes, and he knew what to do with a knife. He attacked with quick movements, cutting and thrusting until he ripped my shoulder open. I caught him with powerful body shots and wore him down. A kick to the chest, followed by some heavy punches to the rib cage, hurt him. I caught him with a roundhouse kick to the head. He went down and stayed there, blood coming from his mouth. A few days later, I heard he had broken ribs, a fractured jaw and a concussion. The other two had broken ribs and one a knackered knee. I had a few bruises, but I needed 35 stitches in my shoulder.

Now, I was a target for the local mobsters. I'd got too close to their racket. The local police came to see me. They asked me to leave under my own terms, or have my visa cancelled. They gave me two days to settle my affairs. New Year's celebrations on Mount Takao were where I said my goodbyes to Yua and family, my martial arts teachers and my Buddhist teacher. He told me he had sensed my restlessness for some time and thought I should follow my heart."

"Eneko, don't postpone your life."

"My friends on the base got me on a military flight out of Japan and, after many stops and changes of planes, I arrived in New York. It was freezing. So I bought a ticket with Cunard and sailed home in style.

So here we are, back in Liverpool!"

Chapter 9 Back to Earth

Begonia stared. "You admire women, don't you? I don't know many men who would ever admit they could learn anything worthwhile from a woman. We must talk again, catch up on our respective pasts. It was a fun evening, Eneko."

Likewise, Begonia had triggered something in me—she had that special something. I knew we'd become friends. You could sense loyalty in her. She would keep her friends close to her. That night, I slept like a log. It had been therapeutic to unload my memories on a sympathetic soul. In the morning, invigorated, I spent an hour working out in my gym. When I entered the office, George had the coffee going, and bagels filled with smoked salmon. I knew George got the coffee from Coopers, but where the bagels and smoked salmon came from was a mystery. In her usual fashion, she lit two Passing Clouds and passed one to me with a cup of coffee and a smoked salmon bagel. She sat down and waited for me to bring her up to date. I spoke for about twenty minutes. She didn't interrupt, just raised an eyebrow and drank her coffee. She was up to speed.

"I got you a date with Begonia," she said.

"A date?" I said.

"Yeah, I bumped into her in Rushworths. We were both looking for Hey There, by Rosemary Clooney. They only had one copy, and I was first.

She used that word you use when you get mad." I laughed and said, "My boss says that all the time.

She laughed, and we got talking. She invited me for a drink. You'd love her car. It's one of those Jowett Jupiter's you love to harp on about. We nipped up to the Philharmonic for a couple of G&T's. And then she drove me home, gave me a great, big kiss and said, goodnight."

I looked at her. She raised an eyebrow or two and said, "Not jealous, are you?"

I ignored the question.

George looked at me with a very serious expression on her face, "Be careful, Boss, she could be trouble."

"Are you seeing her again?" I asked.

"On Saturday. She said she's got some girls over for the weekend."

Chapter 10 Sugar

I called an old school friend who was a Detective Inspector. His nickname was Sugar because of his penchant for sweets.

A tall lanky guy from a tall family. Sugar was 6 ft 5 ins with a long face, a large straight nose, smiling eyes, and a Tony Curtis haircut. Four years my senior at school, he liked football, music, gangster films, dancing, and drinking, but his favourite pastime was chasing women. After leaving school, he joined the Police in the mid-1930s and during the war he became notorious for putting a stop to spivs robbing and beating up sailors on shore leave and relieving them of their fags and rum rations. He would turn up at the spivs's pub, lock the doors, and he and a few tough rozzers would beat them up. That's when Sugar gained the added sobriquet of Lumps.

He was working from The Bridewell in Cheapside today, so we met in the Philharmonic for a pint and then a wander down to Chinatown for a bite to eat. Sugar was fond of Chinese food. The Philharmonic was busy, but we got a table where we could talk.

"You look in shape, still boxing?"

I gave a slight nod in agreement. "You're still as lofty as ever," I said.

"It's the Guinness that keeps you growing, mate," he said.

The pleasantries over, I explained my predicament. He listened, didn't interrupt, even when I mentioned William Mansell and Captain Owens. Sugar drained his pint, then raised his empty glass skywards. The barman nodded and prepared another round. Sugar leaned over and whispered to me that the group was involved in drug and human trafficking and has powerful supporters.

"Eneko, you know the docks are as leaky as a colander, so they get away with murder, literally. Personally, I know they're involved with those evil bastards from the smoke, but it's difficult to prove. And we don't know which officials, or boys in blue, are taking payoffs."

We caught up on old friends and the reds. The barman was holding a phone and pointing towards Sugar. Sugar got up, spoke into the phone, came back, drained his pint and said, "That's me mate, got to go, but I'll be in touch at the end of the week."

Chapter 11 Begonia Has News

Sugar's news left me perplexed. Samurai swords and illegal substances didn't seem to go together. Sounded like another job for George at the library, or maybe me talking to Geoff in Chinatown. I was still daydreaming when I got back to the office.

George looked up. "Anything new?"

"No", she said. I showed her my new Jazz albums, and she looked towards the heavens.

"Philistine," I said under my breath.

"Ears working", she said.

The phone rang. George played secretary, answered the phone, looked over at me and mouthed, "Are you in?"

I mouthed back, "Who?"

She fluttered her eyes and pouted her lips.

"Yes," I said.

George said, "Come on over, Begonia, I'll put the kettle on."

George took a couple of deep breaths. I raised my eyebrows. She started busying herself, arranged her hair, and just for good measure, applied a bit of makeup.

Just as George was putting out the coffee cups and saucers, in walked Begonia. She beamed, kissed George, who looked a bit embarrassed, and kissed me on the cheek and said, "Ah, coffee, any brandy to go with it?"

George went over to the cupboard and produced some glasses and a bottle of Rémy Martin. She poured the coffee, added generous shots of Rémy to the glasses and sat down. Begonia looked terrific. She took off her topcoat, a maroon duffle coat with pale beech-coloured-wooden toggles, underneath she wore a maroon skirt and a beige roll-neck sweater.

"I've got news," said Begonia and produced a large manila envelope from her duffle coat and put it on the table. "That may help you with your inquiry."

She took a large swig of brandy and a sip of coffee, looked up and said, "I'd do the same if I were you."

We sat at the coffee table, and Begonia opened the envelope. Inside were three 10 x 8 black and white photographs: photo number one, two naked men were being whipped by two naked, masked ladies; photograph number two had the taller man with his back to us with a young, masked, skinny boy kneeling in front of him; photograph number three had a naked, statuesque blonde spanking a muscular black lady with a cane.

"Where did you get the photographs?"

"I got them from Kimiko. She was behind a two-way mirror."

"Who the hell is Kimiko?"

She looked me in the eye and said, "She is my half sister."

"Your half sister! How does she fit into the picture?"

"Eneko, it's a long complicated story, it'll take me ages to go through it."

"We're all ears, take your time."

"Okay, I'll try. After my mother died of Spanish flu in 1918, my father met Reiko Kurokawa, whose father, Tetsuhiko Kurokawa, worked for a new Japanese shipping company that wanted to increase trade between Europe and Japan. My parents got married in 1923 and Kimiko was born in '25. My parents spent their time in London, unless my father went to Bilbao to the shipyards. His company had lots of orders in the 1930s but struggled to find materials and I think, although I'm not sure, that they had contacts in the Japanese embassy. In 1935, my grandfather Tetsuhiko Kurokawa retired. He loved London, so he stayed until WW11 started. My father's office moved to Dublin when the war started and he persuaded Tetsuhiko to move to Dublin."

"My father's shipping company transferred him back to Bilbao in early 1942, as the shipyards were getting more and more orders. The family went to Bilbao and settled there. It delighted my stepmother when her father came to stay from Ireland. My stepmother was very close to her father, and he doted on us, Kimiko in particular. We were both good at languages and, of course, we had the perfect opportunity living in London with Spanish and Japanese parents. I stayed in London; after joining the Red Cross; I spent part of the war in London and later in Italy and France."

"So what did you do before the war?"

"I went to the Slade. I did fine arts, but I fell in love with photography and Japanese Art, Manga, in particular. My step mother, Reiko, was a wonderful artist and photographer. She taught me how to draw and to take photographs. She was a real feminist and avid admirer of the works of Florence Farmborough and Olive Edis. I continued to take photos, thousands of them. After the war in early 1947, Tetsuhiko wanted to return to Japan to spend some time in his hometown of Nikko. Reiko and Kimiko travelled with him and spent time there."

George was still looking at the photos. "Do we know who they are?"

Begonia nodded her head, "I do."

"Why was Kimiko there?" I asked. "And where were these photos taken?"

Begonia said, "Kimiko is 8 years younger than me, and when the family moved back to Japan in '46 she couldn't come to terms with living in the countryside. She felt hemmed in. In '47 I began work in Hong Kong for a shipping company through a friend of my father's, and continued with my freelance photography work. I invited her down to stay with me and work in the shipping industry. Kimiko persuaded her mother to let her come and work with me in Hong Kong. The shipping company needed linguists. She was perfect for the job.

"I introduced her to Charlotte, a Dutch national, and a director of her family shipping company. Charlotte knew everybody in Hong Kong and she took a shine to Kimiko. She introduced her to her friends. Kimiko loved it. She liked the people there, life was more exciting than Japan and Hong Kong was booming. It was exciting. Cultural barriers had virtually disappeared, and the nightlife was intoxicating.

"I was doing more and more photography work in Hong Kong, Japan, in fact all over the Far East, so I wasn't around much. I was glad Kimiko had found a friend. Then Kimiko became involved with a Japanese man from Tokyo. He came down to Hong Kong on business, he had money and loved nightclubs and expensive restaurants. He showered her with gifts, introduced her to the joys of illicit drugs. She was young, naïve, gullible, and in love!

"One night when she was out of it, her wonderful boyfriend took some awful staged photos of her with two girls and a soldier. She knew nothing about it until a couple of weeks later when he asked her to organise a party onboard a junk for some wealthy Chinese and

British shipping people. He wanted young girls, European, and Chinese and plenty of drugs and booze.

"Kimiko declined, but then she saw the photos. She knew it would mortify our parents. She didn't know what else to do. That's when it all started: They picked the clients up in separate cars, blindfolded them and took them to a junk, where the party was happening.

"The party area had all the usual accoutrements for fun, drugs, booze, and sex. That's why Kimiko's new job came to the fore. She sat behind a two-way mirror and photographed the action. Some photos were of directors of shipping companies and were used to coerce them to transport merchandise on their ships. They wouldn't know what was on the ships, nor on which ship. They just turned a blind eye."

Begonia looked as if she was about to cry, but she continued, "Kimiko got hooked on opium. I think she did it to blank out what would happen if our family found out. Charlotte supplied Kimiko with drugs, and she knew Kimiko was involved in the shipping owners' coercion plot. But, of course, Charlotte kept herself and her company's ships in the clear. The photos you saw were, I think, of her husband and friend. Two other guys, I don't know, and some Chinese call-girls. The blonde in the other photo was Charlotte. Charlotte asked to try out the party room and loved it. She asked Kimiko to organise a party for some friends, which she did and took some photos, practice shots, if you like. Kimiko thought she recognised Charlotte's husband, but not the friend, and thought no more about it.

"Then out of the blue her boyfriend asked her to find a man called William Mansell who left Hong Kong in 1948 and went to Tokyo and then left in '48/49 for England. Kimiko listened. Her boyfriend had a lot of information about Mansell, his job, his business interests, and his vices. He was married to a Hong Kong based shipping family who were as rich as Croesus. His wife was Dutch and called Charlotte, and she was an opium and sex addict with a penchant for young Chinese girls. Kimiko didn't say that she knew Charlotte or her husband. She knew she was in a real jam and asked me to help, as she didn't know what else to do. It appeared Charlotte came to England in 1951 and she lives in Heswall, on the Wirral. If Kimiko could find the sword, her ex-boyfriend's status would soar in the Yakuza and he said she could leave and take the incriminating photographs with her."

"So they took these photos on the Junk," I said.

"Kimiko said someone took them onboard the Junk in Hong Kong. Kimiko went through all her old negatives and found these."

I said, "That was years ago. How do you know what Mansell is up to now?"

"The same, according to Kimiko, she keeps in touch with Charlotte. And it sounds like he's expanded his budding empire with tie-ups with drug gangs and extortion rackets in London and nationwide and it sounds like he's got some very influential backers. When Kimiko told Charlotte she was coming over to visit, Charlotte was delighted and invited her to stay at her place and organised a cocktail party in her honour. Kimiko had a few drinks with Charlotte and friends at her house. Charlotte was getting eager and asked Kimiko to help her organise her upcoming birthday party, just like old times in Hong Kong. She was as high as a kite, her girlfriends seemed up for it and wanted Kimiko to bring some new, young oriental girls. A real girl-on-girl party, according to Kimiko! Money was no object, she told Kimiko she had a fetish dungeon. Kimiko said the house was a huge sandstone manor with cottages, stables, gardens, and fields for the horses and livestock. Evidently her family has had it for donkey's years.

"Charlotte knew Mansell had a very complicated life in London. He stays married to her for appearances only and when he's up in Liverpool, he either stays at the Adelphi, or the town house in Chester, which Charlotte owns. She knows he won't come to her birthday party as his friends can't stand Charlotte. But she wants to get the dirt on Mansell and some photos of him and his friends in action would get her a divorce and get rid of him for good. And even though he knows she uses drugs, he doesn't know she imports them on her own ships."

I tried to assimilate all this information and keep a clear head. Shouts of "Hello" brought me back from my thoughts. It was Begonia. Begonia and George were in a huddle.

Chapter 12 Begonia Has a Plan

"Okay," said Begonia, "Here's the plan. This Saturday, instead of a party at my place, George and I will get ourselves invited over to see Charlotte and friends. Then we'll get them loaded up with G&T's, they will be stoned as well, we'll get Charlotte to show us her dungeon. And I'll take some photos, discreetly."

"Just like that," I said.

"Yeah, just like that," they said. "Look, Kimiko can spice it up with an offer of some new sex gimmicks from Japan," and she left the rest of the sentence dangling.

I said, "Are you sure?" I got nods. They were laughing their heads off, like they'd won the pools. I tried once more, "What if Charlotte and friends get nasty or horny or both?" I asked.

Begonia looked at me and said, "We can take them on." George blushed, threw Begonia a look. They decided that was enough of me for the day and they departed arm in arm to go for a drink at the Philharmonic.

It surprised me that George looked embarrassed. When she first started working for me, some of her Welsh farming girlfriends used to visit regularly. One weekend they came up to my apartment for some pre-dinner drinks with a girl I'd never seen before, Rhian, who was petite with masses of red hair and a very trim figure. They all inspected the prints on the wall and they loved the Fisherman's Wife print. George said Rhian was the local vet, born in Swansea, and she wanted to see the big city. I took Rhian out for a meal and we got along like a house on fire. After dinner, we returned to my place and George and the girls came round for a drink. But they soon called it night.

Rhian had found the Kama Sutra and was looking at it with more than just idle curiosity. She said, "I'm very supple, but I think I'd struggle with some of these positions. It looks very erotic. George mentioned you had a huge one. I'd love to try it?"

I laughed, took the hint and fired the bath up.

She said, "George is fortunate to have you looking out for her. How long have you been working together?"

"Just over three years."

"And how long have you been in love with her?"

"Just over three years."

Rhian laughed, "Your secret is safe with me, Eneko. Now scrub my back, please."

Chapter 13 A Sumo Wrestler Comes Calling

I went to bed early, hoping that the morning might bring just a hint of sunshine, not just more dreariness. After a hard workout, I showered, dressed, and made coffee. A glance through the window told me it looked worse than ever. An opaque blanket strangling the warmth out of the day. I sat down and poured myself a coffee, my thoughts wandering. A knock on the door broke my revelry. I answered it and was confronted by someone who was taller than Sugar, looked like they built him out of granite, and was as wide as the Three Graces. He walked in, wisps of mist following him. I stepped aside.

He looked down at me and drawled. "It's the kind of weather that calls for coffee and brandy, don't you think?"

I nodded in agreement and stepped into the kitchen, got the coffee machine fired up, grabbed another brandy glass, and put it down next to the bottle of Rémy.

"Help yourself while I make the coffee."

He sat down, poured himself a stiff one, and rolled it around in the glass. He was a veritable giant of a man, at least 6 feet 7 inches, with massive arms and tree trunks for legs. His face was large, with an impressive nose, scar tissue on his wide forehead, warm, dark eyes, and white teeth. His hair was jet black and wavy, which seemed to confirm his ancestry, which was Afro-American and Japanese. He radiated confidence. He was wearing a navy blue Burberry overcoat that was open, and beneath it was a darker blue, double-breasted suit. He'd finished his ensemble with black shoes and a natty Lamont tartan scarf.

I completed my mission of making coffee in silence and delivered it to the coffee table.

I sat down. "How can I help you? "

He looked at me over the edge of his brandy snifter and said, "I want to talk to Kimiko. "

"Kimiko who?" I said.

"Kimiko Kurokawa de Vera Cruz," he murmured, the drawl more pronounced as he relaxed.

"Would you believe me if I said I have never met her?"

"I would, but you know how to find her through her sister, Mr Sora."

"Okay, I'll get her sister to get in touch with you. Do you have a telephone number?"

He reached into his jacket pocket, drew out his wallet, and gave me his business card. "I'm staying at the Adelphi. You can reach me there." He stood up. He towered above me.

"Thank you for coffee and brandy, Mr Sora. I hope to see Kimiko soon."

Chapter 14 Chewing the Fat

After showing him out, I sat down and picked up my bottle of Rémy, or what we'd left of it. And I poured the rest into my empty brandy glass. I looked at his business card: Kaimana Wada, investigator. On the reverse, the same but in Japanese. The name Wada was Japanese, but Kaimana had me at a loss. I suppose he could be from Hawaii. But he was based in Japan and was here looking for Kimiko. Why?

Mr Wada's visit had me perplexed, but if he wanted to harm Kimiko, he wouldn't advertise the fact that he was here and staying at the Adelphi. I needed to talk to Begonia when she finished work.

But putting that to one side, I needed to find out more about Charlotte's house and her devious goings-on. What did she do in Liverpool? Endless questions kept popping into my head. I rang Geoffrey Chang, and I told him I'd see him at the Philharmonic tomorrow evening.

"I've got loads of questions for you to answer."

"You're buying," he said.

I sat down and went through what I'd learned in the last few days. I was still contemplating what I didn't know when the door opened and George sauntered into the office, the weather seeping in after her. She had on a dark tan duffle coat and underneath red trousers with a black sweater—she looked terrific. The coffee maker, my prized Italian, Alfonso Bialetti, was bubbling away.

"Coffee boss?"

"Yeah, please."

We plopped down and gazed at each other quizzically.

"You first."

"Bee doesn't frighten easily."

"Bee?" And then I realised Bee was Begonia —note to self, we are in the 'pool, En.

"Are you with it, boss?"

I nodded, and she continued, "Last night after we left, we jumped in that sports car of hers and zoomed up to the Philharmonic at a nice steady 90 mph. I found a parking space outside the Everyman and sailed into the pub. We got a table just over from the bar, close to a bunch of beards, who were talking skiffle and folk. Jesus, that stuff makes your jazz sound okay. Bee said she really liked the antwacky decor and must see the gent's toilet with its marble interior some time as it's supposed to be ace."

"Antwacky, ace?"

"Yeah, she's really picking up the lingo fast. Anyway, she started telling me about Kimiko and her problems with her ex. He sounds like a typical ratbag that needs to be taken down a peg or two. Bee reckons he's a real popinjay! And Kimiko is keen to get the job done so she can get the sword back to Japan and get her life back on track. Bee said that Kimiko was sure that Charlotte was importing drugs, mostly cocaine and amphetamines, as they were easy to hide. She steers clear of the opium trade, as she doesn't want to get on the wrong side of the Chinese gangs. But strangely enough, the Chinese gangs use her for trafficking young women in for prostitution."

"That's quite a lot of detail in short order. Sometimes remember to take a breath between words!"

I got a sarcastic shrug of the shoulders for my pains.

"I had an interesting visit from a nice guy earlier this morning. A huge guy, about 3 inches taller than Sugar and broader than a ferryboat, I'd say he was a combination of Hawaiian, Afro-American, and Japanese. Polite, to the point of being too polite, well mannered, spoke in a calm, measured voice, and said he's staying at the Adelphi. He left me his card and mentioned that he wanted to talk to Kimiko, and could I arrange it?"

"Wow, we need to talk to Bee now."

Chapter 15 Kimiko's Bodyguard

Thirty minutes later, the office door flew open, and in raced Begonia. She looked ashen. I gave her the business card. She studied it and passed it back to me. "I don't know him."

"Would Kimiko know?"

"Pass me the phone."

She called the hotel, and the conversation went from English to Spanish to Japanese and then settled into a steady stream of Spanish, then sobs and laughter. George looked nonplussed and made more coffee. She opened my secret stash and took out another bottle of Rémy. I gave her a look. She just shrugged and went back to the kitchen.

Begonia looked calmer. Her breathing had slowed as she replaced the phone.

"Bee, there's coffee and brandy on the table. Come and sit down."

Begonia did as she was told. Wrapped up in her duffle coat, she still looked cold. George started lighting Passing Clouds for the three of us and then looked at Begonia.

"Bee, what's going on?"

Begonia took a swig of coffee, downed the Rémy in one gulp, and said, "Good news, I think. Kaimana Wada is one of Kimiko's boyfriend's men from Tokyo. His job was to keep Kimiko safe and secure. Her ex didn't want his very profitable operation put in jeopardy, as Kimiko knew too much."

"So how come Kimiko made it to England?" I asked.

"Eneko, I think her ex knew Kimiko was friends with lots of shipping people and believed she could, with my help, find the missing heirloom, as he had given her the names to trace. They sent Wada to make sure Kimiko kept her part of the bargain and to offer his help if things got rough."

"If things get rough, I'll be happy to have him on our side," I said. "He's a massive guy. He looks like an ex-Sumo wrestler."

"The thing about Kaimana is that I think he's fallen for my sister. And I think Kimiko feels the same about him. He's always stood up for her when her ex was around, and she felt safe with him. Kimiko said that he wouldn't go back to Hong Kong or stay in Japan after they delivered the sword. They plan to get married and live in Honolulu. Can you imagine my little sister living near the beach and swimming every day?"

"Okay, Begonia, I'm glad that Kimiko is feeling safe now that Kaimana is here and confident of getting the sword and the information on Mansell. But be careful, these people sound pretty ruthless to me."

Begonia looked at me and said, "I know, Eneko, I will take care, but can I take George shopping? We need to get some clothes for the party on Saturday. We must look good. Don't worry, this is all the Yakuza's money. When it's gone, it's gone."

That was fine with me. I needed to do a few things and start planning for my meeting with Geoffrey tomorrow.

"Sure, have a good time, and I'll see you later."

They smiled, put on their duffle coats, and swept out into the smog.

Chapter 16 My Liverpool

I decided to go out for lunch. I changed into a midnight blue corduroy suit with a matching waistcoat. I loved my new collection of suits. I used a Hungarian tailor whose shop was in Kensington, an incongruous place for a very specialised tailor who was expensive. I matched it up with chocolate brown shoes, a beige shirt, and a matching chocolate tie. I threw on a dark brown overcoat and beige scarf. I walked out and headed up to the Adelphi.

Lime Street was under an amorphous cloud, with headlights from trams and motor vehicles reflecting off the frost on the pavement. The Adelphi was a one-off. It's slightly over-the-top elegance, with marble pillars and mosaic tiles. I sat down in a quiet corner of the restaurant. The place had a wide clientele, including local or visiting businessmen and people arriving on the Ocean Liners. I started with a crisp Jerez to wash away the lingering coffee taste and settled for a simple lunch, which was excellent, but the cheeseboard was even better, especially with a velvety, strong Port. I sat back and sighed. I loved Liverpool, the wonderful buildings, the trams, the underground, and the docks with all the wonderful liners and cargo ships sailing to the four corners of the earth. But most of all, I loved the people. It was a wonderful mixture of Irish, Welsh, Scottish, Jewish, and, more recently, people from the Caribbean. The cultural and religious differences spawned Scouse humour. It was infectious: if you told a good joke, downed a pint, and enjoyed a laugh, you were all right in Liverpool. And then there was the football: Everton and Liverpool had a proper rivalry. I followed Liverpool because my father was a supporter of La Rioja, so anything red was good! My father was a goalkeeping fan; he adored Elisha Scott, and he used to take me to Anfield, sporting his red Basque beret, when I was very young to see the maestro play.

But back to the present: the business community, local government, and general population seemed caught in a time warp. We had won the war. "Where were the spoils?" seemed to be the mantra, but in the rest of the world, nobody was listening. Our kids still played on bomb sites, ran around in rags, and rationing was still on, like in many old war zones, but the difference was optimism. In Liverpool, there was very little. I had money, so if I needed stuff, I used the black market. My parents had left me a couple of properties that were still intact, a wonderful car, and stocks and shares in various shipping companies; wonderful old Uncle Jesus had also left me his place in Castropol, Spain. I was still lost in my thoughts when a shadow descended over my table. I instinctively reached for my wallet, then I realised it wasn't the waiter with the bill, but Wada San.

He stood there, smiling. Today, he was dressed in a black Haori, a grey Hakama, and matching accessories. A typical traditional Japanese male outfit. He looked even bigger in his native clothing. He nodded, and I asked him to join me for coffee and brandy. He gave a slight bow and sat down. The waiter hurried over, took the order, and disappeared to the bar.

He spoke in a soft voice, "Thank you for contacting Kimiko."

"You are very welcome."

He smiled again. I was beginning to take a shine to this bloke. The waiter hurried back, placed the coffee pot and brandies on the table, gave Wada a smile, and said, "Will that be all, sir?" The waiter obviously knew the wheat from the chaff. Wada nodded, and the waiter hurried off.

Chapter 17 Kimiko Makes an Entrance

Wada looked over my head and beamed. His smile really did light up the room. I turned my head and caught a vision in silk. Kimiko was dressed in a kimono of midnight blue patterned with silver bamboo plants, an obi of light and dark gold, with a bright red motif, and a matching handbag. She looked wonderful, tall for a Japanese girl, with dark, smouldering eyes, a straight nose, and the same mountain of hair as her sister. But her hair was tightly under control to match the calm elegance of her kimono.

I stood up and bowed, and she responded.

Wada said, "Kimiko, this is Eneko Sora, the private detective hired by Begonia."

Kimiko smiled. "Begonia has told me all about you and how much assistance you have been," she said in a very definite home counties accent.

I muttered a reply and sat down.

I didn't know what Wada knew about Kimiko's involvement with the "Pleasure Palace" operation, so I kept my mouth closed and waited for either of them to speak.

Wada said, "Eneko, I have terminated my involvement with the Yakuza. I will return the samurai sword. That's where my responsibility ends, and Kimiko's. We will deliver the sword to them in New York, then Kimiko and I will go to my home in Honolulu. I understand you have all the facts at your disposal, so there is nothing to discuss. I will follow your lead and assist you in any way I can."

Succinct and to the point, I thought, I was going to enjoy working with this calmness. I smiled. The elegantly attired couple were certainly attracting admiring glances and a few furrowed brows.

"Kimiko, you look wonderful and so elegant in your kimono. It reminds me so much of Japan."

Kimiko smiled and said, "Thank you, Eneko; it's my favourite. Kaimana gave it to me for my birthday."

I looked at Kaimana. "You have excellent taste."

He smiled and beamed at Kimiko.

"Do you have any plans for the next few days?"

"No," Kaimana replied.

"Just stay out of sight until the weekend and enjoy the facilities. They have a steam room."

He smiled again. I got up, said my goodbyes, and wandered out into the lobby. I almost walked into Eddie, my boxing coach, at the YMCA. He feigned to throw a left jab and instead shook my hand. He was a good old pro. He'd been around boxing all his life. He still looked in great shape—completely bald and as wiry as they came. We talked about boxing: he had just recently seen Don Cockle and reckoned moving up to heavyweight was doing him no favours. I mentioned I had run into Morris.

"He's still on the door at The Grapes?"

I nodded. And with a "See you at the gym, son," he was gone.

Chapter 18 A Chance Meeting

Geoffrey was already in the Philharmonic when I breezed in. He waved. I got the message and headed to the bar. Another brandy for me and a large G&T for Geoffrey. We shook hands. Geoffrey was about 5 feet 6 inches and getting a bit of a midriff. He looked prosperous in his new Italian suit.

"It's been a while," said Geoffrey. I nodded in agreement. "So, what's on your mind?"

"I've got a fresh case that looks difficult to resolve the more I get to know about it, so I want to fire a few questions at you, mate."

"Shoot away."

"Okay, it's about drugs: opium amphetamines, PCP, cocaine, the whole gambit. They have asked me to find a Japanese sword that's supposed to be here in the UK, brought in via the docks. What I've found out so far is that it's connected to drugs and girls from Hong Kong. Have you heard anything?"

He stared at his glass for a long time. "Yeah, I've heard. To be honest, it's a real pain. The old Chinese opium slurs and labour issues never stop. Eneko, opium was produced here in

Liverpool. It was legal until 1916. Then it became impossible, so they started producing it in Amsterdam and importing it back into Liverpool and other ports, of course. Then, when WW11 kicked off and we had fifteen to twenty thousand Chinese merchant sailors around, it became impossible to control. And after the war, the gangs took over, and then, as you said, it expanded to every drug known to man."

"What about girls and guns?"

"Girls, they sometimes bring young ones as prostitutes, but just a few, too easy for the cops to spot. Guns are a different matter. They import them for their gangs, but there has been a recent movement to supply some of the local white gangs as well."

Great, I thought. This town could turn into Dodge City in a heartbeat.

"So what do the local business people think? Where is the money to be made?"

"Look around, Eneko, lots of restaurants are opening up, the future is food."

I chewed that one over. We had a few more drinks and talked about old times and the present. Geoffrey was now married to a girl we went to school with and had three kids. He lived in Heswall and was enjoying life. He'd even started playing golf. We shook hands again, and Geoffrey left.

I hung around for a while, but it started getting busy and noisy, so I headed home. It had been an interesting day.

Chapter 19 Friday's Plan

In the morning, I was finishing my early workout when the phone in the gym rang. It was George.

"Eneko, Mansell can't make the birthday weekend. He's got some big business meetings in London. So he's going to grace us with his presence midweek, another business meeting with local politicians and crooks, or so says Charlotte. I'm at Begonia's. See you at about noon."

"Fine," I said.

Plenty of time, I thought. So I opened the safe and took out my favourite Beretta, loaded it and fired at the target. Good grouping, still accurate. I cleaned the Beretta and put it back in the safe. The shooting gallery had a vent where any left over discharge went into the sewers. I loved the Beretta, but for real action, I preferred the stopping power of the Browning.

I finished up, got changed into black cords, a crimson wool pullover, and wandered into the office. I fired up the coffeemaker, got some cups and saucers, and sat down. The office door opened, and in walked the three girls. Begonia and Kimiko dressed as male flamenco dancers with bolero jackets, red sashes, matching red hats, and Cuban-heeled boots. Absolutely stunning! George in black culottes with matching boots and a black polo sweater! A game try, I thought.

Begonia spoke, "Morning, Eneko. I don't think tonight is going to be a problem with Charlotte."

I shrugged my shoulders and was about to start talking when George said, "Kimi has a plan, though."

Kimiko smiled and said, "In Hong Kong, we used a junk. But one of our ships is docked at the moment in Birkenhead, taking on freight bound for India. We could use the ship for Mansell and friends, and I could take the photos. We just need to get them there! I could arrange a boys' and girls' night out! He's done it before in Hong Kong."

"And the photos?"

"Not a problem. I'll get one of the crew to fit a peephole in the main cabin. And apart from that, they'll be too stoned to notice."

I said, "So you mean the same routine, black balaclavas, and separate cars?"

"Yeah," said Begonia. "They love all that mystery. It gets them turned on and ready for the kinky stuff."

"But how do we know where they are going to be?" I said.

"Charlotte said that when he comes up to Liverpool for business, he always stays at the Adelphi, and I've checked. He's booked in on Monday, Tuesday, Wednesday, and Thursday nights—four suites in all."

Kimiko chipped in, "I think he's having dinner with Charlotte there on Monday. I could bump into him, get talking, and see if he takes the bait for a kinky night out. If some of the guys want women, that's easily arranged. I'm sure he'll go for it."

"But that's your cover blown," I said.

Kimiko looked at me. "I don't care anymore, and I've got Kaimana to protect me."

Good point, I thought. "Okay, okay," I said. "But make sure you get Charlotte on your side, and make certain she's 100% positive she wants to leave hubby for good. And what about Charlotte? Are you going to try to get the dirt on her tonight as well?"

Kimiko nodded. "I'm taking her two real, tough professionals as a present. When she sees them, her tongue will be hanging on the floor. We'll get her nicely tipsy, and then my friends will pop in for a drink and Hanky Panky time!"

I said, "You look ready to party already!"

George spoke up. "It's a lunch date, so we'll have plenty of time to sort it all out."

"How are you all getting there?" I said.

"George and I are going in my car. Kaimana is driving Kimiko. Do you want to go with them?"

"No, I'll follow you in my car," I said.

Chapter 20 Keeping out of Sight

My car was kept in a lockup in an old cooper's yard at the back of my place. Not much went on in the cooper's yard these days, just old Frank making barrels for Port. He was glad of the rent I paid for my garage space. My car was an Allard J2X in British racing green. It was a real head-turner.

I set off with no particular plan in mind, which was worrying. I thought I'd just sit and wait it out. The girls knew what they were doing. The roads were a little slippy, with left-over sleet and cloying sea mist creating a perpetual murky atmosphere. There was little traffic after we got through the tunnel and headed out towards Heswall. In front, I could see Begonia's car followed by a dark maroon Armstrong Siddeley Lancaster driven by Kaimana. The convoy arrived at Charlotte's house; both cars went up the drive and stopped. The girls got out and went into the house. Kaimana drove out, I flashed my lights, and he parked just over from me on the beachside. I got out and joined him in the Lancaster, a big, beautiful, roomy car. It needed to be.

He looked at me. "This is a real mess," he said.

I was just about to reply when a dark blue Rolls-Royce Phantom 111 swept imperiously through the gates and departed towards Liverpool—nothing unusual in that until I glimpsed Geoffrey at the wheel. He certainly wasn't doing deliveries in that car, or maybe he was.

I replied to Kaimana, "I think you may be right."

"Are you okay with all this and Kimiko's involvement in this racket?"

"No, I'm not, but it is what it is. My job is to get the sword, deliver it, and get Kimiko to the safety of my homeland. In Hawaii, nobody would dare try any reprisals. I know too many people."

"What about the Yakuza? Won't they lose face?"

"No, they get the sword. The rest is just about personal details. The bosses know my position. It's settled."

I couldn't argue with that. If he had friends his size in Hawaii, I couldn't see any problems. We waited. Kaimana had a flask of coffee with him, and he poured out two cups. He was dressed in a regulation navy blue business suit with a matching scarf. He had the aura of a dormant volcano. We talked about Sumo, and it was good to hear his opinions. He even cracked some jokes and smiled a lot. He was very interested in my martial arts training and slapped my knee a couple of times when I made a joke or two in Japanese. It was good; I was enjoying myself.

We waited some more, nothing, then a taxi arrived at the house, and two women got out and entered. I got out of the car, stretched my legs, and lit a cigarette. I offered one to Kaimana, but he shook his head. I was getting tired of waiting. The sea mist was coming in off the River Dee and lying in the gullies at the side of the road, bringing a fine drizzle with it—the kind that soaks you. I climbed back in the car and waited some more. It was now past 5 pm, and the drive was completely obscured. The banks of mist and darkness saw to that. We heard the sound of engines starting up. Begonia's car came out of the drive. Wada flashed his headlights and Begonia slid up to the Rover. "

"Kimiko is at the door, Kaimana," she said.

I jumped out and went to my car, while Kaimana cruised over the main road to the house and picked up Kimiko and the other girls. I clambered into my car and followed them at a discreet distance. My brain was humming, and Geoffrey's name was front and centre.

Chapter 21 The Hangover

I parked the car at Frank's place, reminded myself to get Ted to service the car, walked to the office, which was open, and let myself in. George had coffee and brandy on the go. Both she and Begonia looked a bit bewildered. I kept my peace and waited.

George looked over and said, "Wow, that Charlotte is nuts, completely nuts!" I looked at Begonia. She nodded and said, "George, you present the evidence."

George cleared her throat and sallied forth with the story.

"We got there and were met by the maid who showed us in. Charlotte was already stoned and had the champagne open and chilling. She was naked, she looked sensational, and she really has an amazingly powerful body. Her four friends were playing spin the bottle and were all in various states of undress. She came running over and started kissing everyone and brandishing glasses."

"We all sat down and Charlotte started pouring, and so we started drinking and laughing. I must admit, Charlotte was hilarious and soon started on about her husband and how she needed a divorce as soon as possible. More champagne arrived via the maid, who kept her face as stony as the Sphinx as she filled the ice bucket and lowered in more bottles of fizz. Charlotte's friends were now all naked. It was erotic Japanese sex toy time. Charlotte was nearly out of it and started telling us about her dungeon and her secret staircase. She blabbered on, only stopping when she tried to kiss Kimi and lever her out of her clothes. She could hardly stand up, and she wanted us all to go and try out her kinky stuff in the dungeon. It was getting very tricky. Luckily, the maid stepped in and announced our new guests: two beautiful, slim Chinese girls."

Kimi introduced them as Jackie and Sarah. Our birthday present.

"Charlotte licked her lips. The girls smiled and kissed her. Jackie slapped Charlotte hard on the rear end, and she said play time and nodded at us. They grabbed a very receptive, naked Charlotte and left the room. We knew she'd gone to her dungeon, so we waited. Bee led the way to the dungeon, camera at the ready. By the time we arrived, the girls had Charlotte bound and strapped to a bench. Jackie was really whipping Charlotte's bottom with a bamboo stick. There were big, red marks on her arse. Kimi had the door ajar, and the camera was ready. We didn't stay long, just long enough to get some very racy photos. We waited in the lounge for what seemed like a long time until Jackie opened the door and asked Kimi for some help. We went down to the dungeon, got the naked and now unconscious Charlotte into a dressing gown, and carried her back to the lounge."

"We got her settled and rang for the maid. She didn't turn a hair; she said she'd put her to bed with some help. After that, we left. Her friends were still asleep in the lounge. The maid took it all in her stride, another day at Charlotte's house."

I looked up and said, "Have you got somewhere to keep the photographs and negatives safe?"

Begonia shook her head, and I replied, "Not to worry, I have the use of a darkroom. There is no need for any outside help."

Begonia smiled and handed me her camera. "Black and white Kodak Tri X," she murmured.

"No problem, I'll do them tomorrow."

George refilled the brandy glasses and sat down. "Wow! That was an education. Is all that stuff made in Japan and Hong Kong?"

"Mostly," said Begonia. "Kinky is here to stay."

"Is Kimiko going to take the photos on the ship?" I asked?

"Yes, let's keep to the plan," said Begonia.

"Okay, I'll leave that with you, but Kaimana and I will be in close attendance, for sure."

The girls looked exhausted. George said, "We'll sleep in my place tonight."

I said, "Good night."

Chapter 22 All Aboard

The weekend would give me time to sort out the photos, make arrangements for next week's exciting adventure—just another normal week. I was thinking about a snack and another Rémy when the phone rang. It was Sugar.

"Eneko, sorry to ring so late, but I've been manic all week."

"No problem; the life of a crime fighter is never easy."

"You're not kidding, pal. I've had a bit of a breakthrough--that Captain Owens you mentioned is skippering a ship that's due in on Wednesday night, or early Thursday. It loaded up in Hong Kong, then docked in Panama and New York before heading here. It appears it picked up three passengers in New York. That's all I know."

I took a deep breath before I replied. I couldn't mention the operation Kimiko was running, that would put the whole deal in jeopardy.

"Sugar, you're going to have to trust me on this one. I've got an investigation going on that's probably going to put Mansell and Owens in the frame, but I need until Tuesday or Wednesday at the latest. But definitely before Owens's ship docks. I think you'll need backup. There could be a few of them."

"Okay, Eneko, but don't get too clever. These guys are dangerous with a capital D. Keep me up to speed. I'll call you on Wednesday morning."

I poured another Rémy. This is going to be tight, I thought. If Kimiko doesn't make the right connection.

My plan was very simple: I'd prepare two envelopes for Mansell, one with the incriminating photos of his in flagrante delicto; the other with photos of the sword. I would explain that I was acting on behalf of a client who would like the exchange to be made as soon as possible; otherwise, these photos could be forwarded to the relevant authorities. As an added touch, I'd prepare a letter from my client in Japanese with a Hanko signature stating that I, the interlocutor, had no knowledge of the contents of either envelope. The exchange was to be conducted in the confines of the safety deposit room in one of the main Liverpool banks; two boxes had been reserved, one for each party. Once both parties were satisfied, the matter was terminated. Kaimana would be my client's authenticator.

I developed the photos. Charlotte had the body of an athlete, despite the way she lived. Her torso was muscular, and her breasts defied gravity. And her thighs and buttocks looked powerful. I bet she could be a real handful. But she was a mess. Someone needed to lend her a helping hand.

The photos could be of some use, but I didn't think Kimiko would need them to persuade Charlotte to help out. She seemed desperate to leave Mansell. Kimiko could always give Charlotte the old photos from Hong Kong as a threat if needed. But I bet Mansell would have bigger problems to worry about. If the photo session on the ship went according to plan, we would be out of the woods. And as soon as Kaimana witnessed the exchange and took the sword, he and Kimiko should beat it fast. The probable drug shipment on Thursday and the heavy mob from London would be my problem and Sugar's.

Chapter 23 The Quiet before the Storm

The weekend passed like a day in the dentist's waiting room. I made sure I had enough solutions and photographic paper for next week, checked that my pistols were ready to go, and practised some Kendo in the gym. I treated myself to dinner at the Mecca in North John Street on Saturday night, a good excuse to wear my new scarf. There weren't many customers. The pea soup weather was the perfect excuse to stay home, and I couldn't blame them. Walking back to my place, the streets were deserted. The only sounds were the squeals of steel tram wheels.

I got back home about 9:30 pm and decided to enjoy a Rémy while listening to Django Reinhardt and the band. It was my father who got me interested in jazz. He loved it, especially when combined with gypsy music. He adored Stephane Grappelli's violin and went to see him most years before the war. He would get his Ariel Square Four 4F motorbike out and head off to The Quintette du Hot Club de France in Paris and live jazz for a weekend. It had rubbed off. I settled down to an evening of jazz, but my thoughts soon wandered to Kimiko and if she could swing this little party onboard the ship in Birkenhead. Did she have the cars, the girls, the booze, and the drugs?

I decided to sleep on it.

Sunday was a washout; it poured with rain, but at least the air was clearer. I called Ted and said I'd drop the car off at his place if that was okay. He said he'd meet me at the Gardener's Arms, and I could grab the tram back. I drove up, had a pint with Ted, and caught up with all the news about cars, taxis, and spare parts. I jumped on the number 6 tram, which dropped me back in town, missing the torrential downpour. Later in the afternoon, the phone rang. It was Sugar.

"The ship's due to dock at Huskisson, so we can wait in Sandon or Canada. It should give us a good line of sight."

"What about using Tate & Lyle as a watchtower?"

"Already sorted.

"Okay, but I hope you've got a weather report."

"Yeah, heavy mist, followed by fog and more fog." He rang off.

I'd just put the phone down when it started ringing. It was George. She said Bee had spoken to Kimi after speaking with Charlotte. Charlotte was desperate to help. She planned to have drinks in the cocktail bar with Mansell and cronies, bump into Kimi where Kimi would be having drinks with four or five of her girls, then let Kimi weave her magic with Mansell and his associates.

George sounded very confident. I said, "Goodnight."

Chapter 24 Cocktails for One and All

Monday dawned. I opened the office door and could see Cooper's yard peeping out of the mist. That was an improvement. The phone rang, and George answered, "No, Eneko hasn't arrived yet. I'll get him to ring you when he gets in."

I raised an eyebrow. "Bernie," she said.

I could do without that right now, so I made a mental note to call him later. I hated waiting around. My initial instinct was to get Kaimana and pay Mansell a visit, but that had disaster written all over it, so I waited. George was keeping herself busy catching up on some typing and filing away papers, but she was in automatic mode. I went and made us coffee, lit two Passing Clouds and said, "A penny for 'em?"

"What?"

I raised my eyebrows. I was getting good at this. George gave me a little lob-sided smile.

"I'm getting worried about what's going to happen in the next few days. Kimi seems okay, but Bee is getting close to panic stations."

"You should take Begonia to the flicks tonight. The Quiet Man is still playing—a nice romantic comedy that should help Begonia with her Irish!"

George laughed. "That's the best idea you've had for ages. Who'll be the lady of the house?" She giggled. "Boss, when this crap is all over, can I take a break, a short one, to sort myself out?"

I nodded, bent over, and kissed her on the cheek. She gave me a quizzical look. "75% Spanish, remember?" I said.

I called Bernie. He was fretting badly. "Eneko, you know what has hit the fan? The mob is coming around on Saturday to see our association and fix the price for the whole jewellery trade in the city. What the hell do we do?"

"Put them off until Tuesday. I'm busy this weekend. Where and when?"

Bernie explained, in great detail, the location and who was going to attend. I replied and told him to stop worrying, and I'd get it sorted.

"But what about the guns?"

"Don't worry about guns; we can match that."

I put the phone down.

George looked over. "You got a gun, then?"

I tapped my nose with my forefinger. She laughed.

I decided to take a bath, so I let it run and went back to the office.

"Bath time?"

"Can I join you; be Japanese for a while."

"Absolutely."

I showed George the ropes, cleaning myself thoroughly before getting into the bath to soak. It was hard not to stare. She looked in great shape, with a lovely figure and beautiful skin. She climbed into the bath to soak, and I joined her.

"This is wonderful. The Japanese know how to relax. And I did look; you are really very muscular, good husband material!"

"Are you proposing?"

George laughed. "I think you are the only man that's ever seen me naked."

"Isn't this where I say we can't keep meeting like this?"

She splashed me, put her head back, closed her eyes, and let the hot water work its magic.

Chapter 25 The Mice Come out to Play

The phone rang, and I climbed out of the bath and answered.

"Hi Eneko, it's all fixed for tonight. I'm going to be there with Kimiko. Charlotte was playing along and seemed stone-cold sober and very serious."

"Okay, Begonia, but it might be an idea to get Kimiko to keep Kaimana out of the way tonight."

"I agree. Is it okay if George keeps me company?"

"Sure, but be careful. If it looks like trouble, just bail out."

George had followed me into the office. I handed her the phone, and they had a lengthy discussion before George hung up.

I looked at George. "Right, I'll be in the hotel. You won't see me, but if you do, it means the game's up. Just grab Begonia and leave fast."

George nodded. "Bee's coming for me in 15 minutes. I hope not to see you later."

I grinned. George quickly dried her hair and put her bathrobe back on. A car horn sounded.

George grabbed a bag, kissed me, and skipped out.

I picked out a black overcoat under which I dressed in a plain black suit, grey shirt, black shoes, and glasses. The air was damp, but there was no rain, just the ubiquitous mist. At the Adelphi, I went into the foyer, deposited my overcoat in the cloakroom, and went into the bar. A seat behind a pillar concealed me from prying eyes. After catching the waitress's eye, I ordered a large Rémy and a coffee. So, armed with drinks and a copy of the Times in front of my face, I settled down to wait.

Begonia arrived with George and Charlotte, and they headed into the bar. Charlotte was dressed to kill—a red, silk dress almost backless and matching shoes. She was a head-turner. Begonia was wearing her Flamenco outfit again, and George had tight, fitting black pants and a yellow blouse with matching very high heels. She definitely caught the eye; she must have been about 6 feet 2 inches.

The foyer suddenly looked fuller. Mansell and his four associates had landed. They were all in tuxedos; three of them looked like bodybuilders on a night out. Mansell's smile had all the warmth of an alligator. Charlotte came out to greet them. There were lots of smiles as they entered the cocktail bar. I sneaked a peek, and Charlotte was introducing the girls. The muscle men certainly looked impressed. I waited patiently, and then Kimiko and five girls arrived:

two tall blonde girls, two very elegant Chinese girls, and a black girl in a dress that she must have been poured into; Kimiko in a high-collar Chinese jacket of red and gold and matching red pants. Wow! What a bunch, They looked amazing. As they entered the bar, heads turned, and the background chatter diminished for a moment. Charlotte took centre stage as the girls were introduced and glasses were raised.

The booze flowed. There was no sign of anyone going for dinner. Another group arrived. They were part of a band that was playing in town, just getting in tune for tonight's gig. I thought another hour of this and no one would be standing. I looked up again, and Charlotte was in the foyer with Mansell, and they appeared to be chatting quite amicably. Mansell looked very excited. Charlotte looked at him and rubbed her thumb and forefinger together. Mansell chortled, and I caught the words, "Tomorrow at 8 pm it is."

Charlotte, Mansell, and associates left the bar and went towards the dining room. Kimiko's harem blew kisses and left by taxi. Kimiko kissed George and Begonia good night and disappeared upstairs to the safety of Kaimana. George and Begonia had a cab waiting, but I decided to walk. The frost clung to the lamp posts while the mist lifted from the cobbles at every step, but the cold air cleared my head.

The phone was ringing as I opened the office door. I grabbed it; there was a slight hesitation, then Begonia spoke up, "Sorry, I thought you hadn't answered."

"I just made it. How did it go?"

"What a bunch of pigs."

"What did you expect?"

"Jesus, Eneko. They were utterly disgusting; any qualms I had have flown away. Kimi was brilliant; she had them eating out of her hand, and Charlotte was superb. She kept saying, You deserve a good time, Mansell. "I've been such a bitch, etc."

"So 8 pm tomorrow, then?"

"Yes, but, hey, how did you know?"

"I've got big ears."

"Yeah, Kimiko has got everything prepared: cars, blindfolds, girls, kinky stuff, booze, and drugs. She's going to be the organiser, so she needs to be around; I'll take the photos."

"No, you bloody well won't. I'll be there, taking them. Kaimana will be onboard to assist if necessary."

"Are you sure?"

"100% positive."

"What I want you two to do tomorrow is talk to Charlotte, see if she knows the names of those charmers tonight, and where Mansell's place is in Chester."

"Okay, I'll find out."

"Can you put George on?"

George answered. I told her to keep calm, follow Begonia's lead, and get the information out of Charlotte at all costs.

"Okay," she said.

"Oh!" Bee said, "What about a camera?

"Don't worry; see you later."

Chapter 26 Calling in a Favour

After a hard session in the gym, I checked my cameras, loaded the film, and took extra film just in case. I took the Beretta and the Browning Hi-Power out, checked them, loaded them, and put them in my camera case. I stowed one of my own swords in a sports bag, and I was ready.

I made a call and met Binns at the White Star for a pint at lunchtime. Binns was a safecracker, one of the best in the business. I ran into him when he broke into a safe in some mansion and found a lot of nasty photos of kids and a good deal of folding money. He knew Ted from the war, so Ted put him on to me. I got the evil bastards sorted out, and they got put away for a long spell in Walton Jail. Binns and I split the money, and I kept the safe cracking exploits to myself. Binns was definitely ex-army, and as Welsh as they come, I'd heard he was a bit of a legend in the valleys of North Wales.

Binns was strolling down Matthew Street as I reached the door to the White Star. The Army and Navy stores couldn't have had a better advertisement for their wares: a regulation army duffle coat, army boots, and cap. He was in his early forties, 6 feet, lean with brown hair and hazel eyes, and when he spoke, he sounded like he'd just stepped off the welsh hills. He was smoking his favourite Craven A. We shook hands. His fingers were long and had brown nicotine stains, courtesy of his love for tobacco.

We exchanged hellos and entered the pub. Maisy was serving behind the bar. She nodded to a table in the corner and brought over two pints and put them on the table.

"There's a job I need to do tonight, but I won't know the exact location until this afternoon, except that it's in the centre of Chester."

I pointed to my sports bag on the floor.

"In the bag is a Japanese Samurai sword. It's a copy of the real thing, which is in a safe in the study. I imagine it will be in a long cloth bag; just replace it and bring home the real McCoy."

He nodded, "Shouldn't be a problem. "

"Be careful, mate; these are really dangerous bastards from the smoke, and they're ruthless as hell."

"I'll be well prepared, mate; old habits are hard to break. I've got a couple of jobs to do at my workshop. Call me when you've got the details."

I slid the sports bag over. "The details are in the envelope, all as white as snow."

He laughed, finished his pint, and left.

The phone rang, Maisy picked it up, spoke a few words, and said, "That was me, old man, on the blower; he reckons the fog's going to be bad tonight."

On my way back to the office, I glanced up at the rooftops, and Masie's old fella was right. The chimney pots on all the buildings had already disappeared. I made a coffee, decided against a Rémy, and waited.

At about 3 pm, the phone made its usual drone. I answered, and George started speaking at about 100 mph. "Whoa, slow down, George, take a deep breath."

10 seconds of silence, then George gave me the Chester address. And also that Mansell has no people living in his house. Just his pride and joy of an alarm system for security. She also named the London gang.

"Well done, George."

I called Binns and gave him the address and the news about the alarm system.

He said, "The weather forecast is looking good for me; no problem; meet you in the White Star at lunchtime tomorrow."

I replaced the receiver, opened a fresh pack of Passing Cloud, lit one, and thought about how I was going to keep Sugar up to date without him jumping the gun and upsetting my apple cart.

There is no point in beating about the bush. I dialled his number, and he answered.

"Shaw here."

I told him things were looking good for Thursday, and I had some names for him. I reeled all the names off, making sure I'd got them right.

"Jesus Eneko, you've hit mob royalty."

"Sugar, just bear with me, and we should be able to catch them all with their pants down. I'll call you tomorrow with all the latest dirt and hopefully how they are planning to get to the ship and unload the merchandise."

"Okay, mate, I'll wait for your call."

Chapter 27 Lights, Camera, Action

Wada was waiting at the rear entrance of the Adelphi as I drove up. He levered his body into my car; I'd already moved the seat back as far as it went. He said, "Kimiko and her girls were already in their suite, getting the guys primed for their big night. Plenty of Champagne cocktails, concocted by Kimiko, with some added extras. The girls got the guys changed into pyjamas with big fluffy dressing gowns and gold masks."

At the rear of the building, they had already organised the exit. Three Rolls-Royce Silver Dawns, hired especially for the occasion that came with chauffeurs, were purring. After the girls got their charges in the limos, the vehicles were swept away. The girls were to keep talking until they were onboard the vessel.

The fog was relentless as I drove towards the Mersey tunnel. In the tunnel, we had some respite, but once out in the Wirral, the conditions were just as bad. I headed for the dock where the vessel was berthed. The windscreen wipers were struggling to keep any worthwhile view of the road. Slowing to a crawl, we entered the dock. On a night like this, no one was lingering. The water looked filthy, cold, and oily —not somewhere you'd want to go for a paddle. I took my bag out of the boot and headed for the ship. The breeze was rustling the rigging, and the fog and frost clinging to the ship's superstructure made it look like a ghost ship.

The gangway looked slippery and icy. No one was about, but then, out of the gloom, someone gestured for us to follow. He moved like a cat, only slowing down when we reached an open cabin door. He opened it, showed us in, and then took his leave. The cabin was bare except for two wooden chairs. Near the corner of the cabin, the crew had made a peephole. Through it, I could see a room with wall mirrors, whips, and all the wonders of the sex trade.

I emptied my bag, put the cameras on the table, and pulled out the hardware.

Wada grunted as I gave him the Browning.

"My favourite," he said.

"Did you use one in the army?"

"I spent time in the military, mostly in Europe, but I made it to Japan in 1946. I got stuck in Okinawa for a while, but when they found out about my background, Hawaiian/ Japanese, and that I spoke Japanese fluently, some bright spark transferred me to Tokyo to help with translating and stuff."

"Then in '48, my time was done, but I stayed and got in with the local Yakuza, nothing heavy, just liaising between them and the boys in uniform. Cigarettes, booze, uppers and downers, just random stuff. Then, in '50 or thereabouts, I got asked to look after Kimiko in Hong Kong in case anything went wrong with the parties on the junk. The living was easy, until one time in Hong Kong some idiots kicked off and started beating up the girls, Kimiko included, so I waded in and settled the problem."

"For the next few days, Kimiko kept glancing at me but saying nothing. Then one night she wanted to go to dinner on Hong Kong Island, so I drove her up to the top. We found a restaurant with a view of the harbour, had dinner, and we were talking when she blurted out the entire story—the photos, the drugs, her boyfriend."

"That must have come as a surprise," I murmured.

"Yes and no, but she wouldn't let me do or say anything. Kimiko got in touch with Begonia, who was absolutely furious with her ex-boyfriend, the budding Yakuza, but common sense prevailed, and we bided our time."

"Then they asked Kimiko if she could find the blade. She told Begonia, who found out about Mansell and the ship via her contacts in the shipping world. She was the one who came up with the plan for her ex-boyfriend. You get the blade, and Kimiko goes free. The ex and the Yakuza agreed solely because they would gain a lot of prestige."

I told him my plan for getting the sword tonight. He gave me a shrug and a smile. I couldn't tell if it impressed him, so I also mentioned the changeover and him authenticating the blade. He beamed at that.

A steel door clanged, and we could hear girlish laughter and the whoops of male testosterone. We waited, and nothing happened. I looked at Kaimana.

"The girls, including Kimiko, have delivered the party to the larger cabin behind that hatch over there."

Lifting a giant forearm, he pointed across the room to a metal hatch. Kaimana continued, "In the cabin, the party will have had their masks removed to find 10 masked girls, completely naked. That's why all the whooping and hollering."

The sounds of whatever the hell was going on in there continued and then suddenly stopped. The hatch in the cabin in front of our hidey hole opened, and four naked, masked girls dragged a completely spaced-out Mansell, who was grinning like a baboon; he looked like a total mess. I almost felt sorry for the guy. One of the girls whispered in Mansell's ear, and he started laughing. The metal hatch opened again, and a tall black guy, oil glistening on his body, walked into the cabin. The girls were clapping, cheering, and slapping Mansell, who, by the look of him, was in another world. I snapped off a whole roll of Tri-X and started to pack my things away.

Wada nodded, and we departed. Once on deck, the same guy who met us pointed the way to our car.

Inside the car, the view was just like looking at a white wall. A deathly silence cloaked the docks. Now and again, fog horns coming from the river broke the night's quiet.

"No need for masks. They would never find this place again," said Kaimana.

"The girls are going to need help to get that lot back to the hotel rooms."

"They and some of the crew will get them back in the bathrobes; they'll be driven to the rear door at the hotel, and Kimiko has arranged for the reception staff to ignore the returning party. Then in the morning, after the hangover, they'll probably remember very little except that they had a great time."

"What the hell did Kimiko give them?" I asked.

"All kinds of weird stuff—including a drug the US military was using during the war."

We drove back in silence; the fog was covering everything. Thank God we got a break going through the Mersey Tunnel. At the Adelphi, Kaiamana slipped out of the car.

I said, "I hoped to have the exchange on Thursday morning."

He just nodded in his usual manner and passed me the Browning. I said, "keep it for now."

Driving back to my place was a nightmare; the street lights were worse than useless. God! I needed a shower to get the fog out of my hair and the filth out of my head!

Chapter 28 The Art of Developing

The next morning, I spent very little time in the darkroom. It was very straightforward. Mansell was cooked. Homosexuality was still a crime, even in 1954.

I went back upstairs, and the phone rang. It was George.

Before she had a chance to say anything, I said, "It went according to plan. I've just finished developing the film." She relayed the message to Begonia, who I heard yell, "Great."

Before I could add anything, Begonia came on the line, "Brillant, Eneko. Everything is good with Kimiko. The super studs are all tucked up in bed with a big hangover."

"Okay," I said, "Now listen: I want Kimiko and Kaimana booked on a flight out of here on Thursday evening; Kaimana will have the sword. I don't care where they fly to; just do it. I also want you and George to leave town on Friday morning for a week or so. Go to George's family's place in Wales, okay?"

Begonia said, "Are you okay?"

"I am," I said, "but I'll be even better when you two leave town. Get George to ring me next week."

"Okay," she murmured.

I looked at my watch, an hour before my meeting with Binns. I showered, got dressed in black, to match my mood, and stepped out into yellow daylight—not sun but sulphur.

I skated over the cobbles. My new shoes, with brand new leather soles, were acting like ice skates.

Maisy was on duty, as usual. She said, "Eneko, my sister told me what happened at her place. You okay?"

I said, "Yeah, don't worry, I'll sort it out later."

"I know she can act like a real cow, but deep down, she's got her heart in the right place."

She held up two pint glasses and nodded to the snug. Binns was dressed in his usual sartorial elegance, with a Craven A smouldering between his fingertips. He looked pleased with himself. Maisy arrived and delivered the beer. We each supped a bit.

Binns pointed to the sports bag.

I said, "All present and correct?"

Binns said, "And some. I got to his gaff a little after 7 pm. The fog wasn't too bad in Chester. I parked up out of sight of the house and did a recce. Deserted, it didn't look like anybody had been there for a while. I went around the back and checked out his alarm system. Pretty standard stuff. I entered through a kitchen window, easy access, and simple to cover my tracks."

"No problem finding the safe?"

"None at all; he probably thought he was smart for putting it behind a mirror in his office. It took me a while. It was quite a decent old safe, but easy enough if you know how. I opened it up —no sword, and I was just about to shut it when something caught my eye. Next to a large bundle of cash was a cardboard folder. In it were some really dodgy photos of guys and kids. And next to that was a journal with numbers and deliveries of drugs, names, and places. I had another look around but saw nothing, so I replaced everything."

"I figured there had to be another safe, so I sat down and surveyed the room, it didn't feel right. There was a photo in the middle of a big portion of the wall. It looked out of place, so I checked, and under the photo was a button that opened up a concealed passage with an office on one side and a door on the other side that led to the garage."

"Inside the office were a small desk, a phone, a filing cabinet, and various pictures on the walls. It seemed much smaller than it appeared from the outside. I measured the outside dimensions against the interior ones—a big difference. After about 15 minutes of searching, I found a lever inside the bookcase. The bookcase swung open to reveal a big old

Milner safe. There was nothing in there except the sword. I exchanged them and was about to move out when I heard muffled voices coming from the front of the house."

"I moved back up the passage and heard things being dropped on the floor, then a voice. 'Okay, let's go to the pub. We can sort out this lot later.' I gave it ten minutes, then locked everything up, made sure there was nothing out of place, went back out the way I came, put the gear in the car and went to the pub. I heard the same voices in the bar: Cockneys—three of them, big, hairy bastards. So I left them to it."

"Would you recognise any of them again?"

He looked at me, took another drag on his Craven A, reached into his pocket, and put a Minox Riga miniature camera in front of me.

"Everything in the safe is on there, plus a few snaps of the ugly mob and the car's registration numbers. Are you okay with developing them?"

"Jesus H. Christ, just what did you do during the war?"

"That's another story, Eneko, another story. I enjoyed it, and it brought back some memories. Let me know how it goes."

And with that, he sauntered out. He had a broad smile on his face.

Chapter 29 Catching my Breath

Racing home, I nearly fell three times on the bloody cobbles.

I opened the office door and locked it carefully behind me. I didn't want any unwanted disturbances while I went through the sports bag. I opened the bag, and there it was, the Go Yoshihiro Nagasa styled 14 Century blade—deadly and beautiful. It was a family heirloom anyone would be proud of. Carefully replacing it in its cloth bag, I took it down to the gym with everything else. Binns' night's work took a while to develop. I couldn't afford any mistakes, as these photos were dynamite. The negatives were crisp and clear, so after drying them, I made prints of everything.

The kids' and adults' photos were stark—what a bunch of disgusting bastards. If ever a group needed sorting out, this group did. Reading through the journal, I came to the conclusion that Mansell was an idiot, or so far up himself, he thought he was untouchable. The Cockney thugs I didn't recognise, but I'm sure Sugar could put names to faces.

But why were they here? It must be for the drugs—it was too much of a coincidence not to be. The gang must be picking up the drugs from Mansell's place. The Cockney mob must be carrying a load of cash!

First, I called the hotel; I asked for Wada. Kimiko answered, "Hi Kimiko, could I speak to Kaimana?"

Kaimana said, "What's up?"

"A change of plan, my friend. I'm coming to see you with the blade now. I want you and Kimiko out on a plane and flying out today."

"What about the exchange tomorrow?"

"I have thought that over. You don't need to be there. Remember, I'm acting on behalf of a client. We don't need to complicate things, okay?"

"Whatever you say, Eneko."

I put the blade in the sports bag and caught a taxi on Victoria Street to the Adelphi. Kaimana was at the suite door when I arrived. Kimiko was looking slightly apprehensive, so I put the bag on the floor and took out the blade. I thought Kimiko was going to burst into tears, but instead she controlled herself, hugged me, and kissed me on both cheeks—very Spanish today.

"Right, get the first flight out of here, but ring Begonia, tell her your change of plan, and ask her to call me this evening."

Kimiko nodded and bowed.

Kaimana said, "Good working with you, Eneko."

I smiled and said, "Maybe I'll visit you in Hawaii some time."

"Eneko, you're welcome to our home anytime."

I opened the door, Kaimana stopped me and dropped the Browning in my overcoat pocket. He grinned.

I closed the door behind me, Sayonara, I murmured to myself.

I went down to reception and left my card with a message for Mansell to call me very urgently. I also gave the receptionist two enclosed envelopes, one with a photo of last night's extravaganza in a plain brown, sealed envelope. The other was a plain white, sealed envelope with a photo of the sword.

I called Sugar. He was out. I left a message for him to come round to my place any time this evening. My trap was laid. I didn't care if Mansell checked the sword in his safe. I doubt he'd notice the difference, and if he did, he was hardly likely to tell me.

Chapter 30 Telephone Calls

I made a sandwich and a strong black coffee and sat down to wait. The phone rang: "Sora, speaking."

A loud, threatening stream of invectives came racing down the line and came to an abrupt stop.

"Sorry, are you sure you have the right number?"

"Listen, mate, I want all the photos and the negatives; do you hear?"

"Am I speaking to Mr Mansell?"

"Yes."

"Mr Mansell, I am acting on behalf of a client who asked me to leave the envelopes for you. As you understand, I have absolutely no idea what is in either envelope. Another large envelope is in my possession, which I am to exchange for something you have in your possession."

"Let's make it tomorrow morning, somewhere out in the open," he barked.

"Tomorrow morning at 10 am would fit in with my schedule perfectly. Should we say the Seacombe Ferry at 10 am?"

"You'd better bring the lot," he snarled.

"How will I recognise you?"

"How will I recognise you?"

"Ah! Yes, of course, I'll be wearing a beige Burberry trench coat and carrying a beige, calf-skin briefcase."

I thought that went better than expected. He sounded like a total moron. Plenty of time for a coffee and an Ella Fitzgerald album.

Chapter 31 Coffee with Sugar

I loved Ella. It had been a while since I had time to listen to those dulcet tones. The doorbell interrupted my musical interlude. A tall figure was casting a shadow into the office. It must be Sugar.

I opened the door. "Come in and take the weight off," I said.

"Thanks, Eneko."

"Coffee, Rémy," I said.

"Sounds good."

I brewed up, measured out two very large Rémys, and plonked them down on the table.

"You look like the cat who got all the cream."

"How would you like to get yourself promoted?"

He took a slurp of Rémy and a sip of coffee and said nothing.

"Okay, pin your ears back and listen to my enchanting tale of modern crime."

I ran him through my litany of lies and half truths about how I got possession of some really nasty and interesting stuff. He looked at the kid's photos, and his eyes almost pierced through the paper. I continued before he could interrupt and placed photos of the ledger and banknotes in front of him.

"Can I borrow these, Eneko?" he asked.

"They are all yours, pal. But I'm saving the pièce de résistance until you finish your Rémy, because I need another one."

Glasses filled, I took out the photos of the London villains and placed them on the table.

"Jumping Jesus Almighty!" Sugar yelled.

"Do you know them?"

"Know them. Every drug squad officer knows these bastards."

"Okay, now listen up, and I'll tell you what I know. The guys I showed you the other day, we think, are bringing the drugs in. This loveable bunch is staying at Mansell's place in Chester. I think they are the money men and are waiting for the drugs to arrive before paying up and heading back to London. I can't tell you how I got this stuff, but if you could nab them red-handed in Chester, you'll have them all. I know Chester is not your patch, but…"

Sugar was way ahead of me. "No problem. I work with an old mate in Chester. We went through training together. We're pretty tight. Where the hell was this stuff? Don't tell me it was just lying around."

"No, it's in his safe. Don't ask, okay?"

"We can't use that as evidence."

"I know."

He looked at me and said, "Jesus Eneko, what am I going to do with you?"

He leaned back in the chair, downed his Rémy in one, and looked at me again. "Okay, so you think we should let the drugs leave Liverpool and follow the gang to the house in Chester? I'll have a warrant ready, which won't be a problem because one of those choirboys is wanted for importing drugs and weapons from Amsterdam."

"More or less, the gang who are left at the dock could be picked up later. You know where they are. You just need some coppers who are good at keeping under cover."

"Okay, I need to get organised. I'll get my Chester mate onboard and my team ready for Thursday night. In the meantime, I'll get people on the kiddy filth. They'll be able to put names on faces. The Chief will love that. I've also got a WPC who's dynamite with accounts and numbers. If it's findable, she'll find it."

"Sugar, remember, these clowns are armed and ready to go."

"You're a star, Eneko. Make sure you keep your head down."

I made a sandwich. The phone rang again. Begonia yelled, "I love you. You've saved my little sister."

"Begonia, a change of plan: I want you two gone tomorrow morning. Go to George's place in Wales, hide out in the hills, and talk to the sheep, or something. This should all be over by Sunday, so ring me on Monday, okay?"

I hung up. I didn't want any more arguments or discussions.

Chapter 32 The Double Cross

Thursday morning came, and with it more mist that was forecast to turn to fog later. I made myself a coffee, some toast, and smoked a couple of Passing Clouds.

I dressed in a dark brown corduroy suit, beige roll-neck sweater, and dark-brown brogues. I put on my beige Burberry Trench Coat, which had two large pockets with ease of access. I put my Beretta in the right-hand pocket, leaving my left hand free to carry the briefcase. In the briefcase, I put a sealed, large brown envelope.

I put on my trilby, checked the time, 9:30 am, stepped out onto the shiny, wet cobbles, and hailed a cab on the corner. The cabbie, a football fan, gave me chapter and verse on how Liverpool was going to stave off relegation this season. I mumbled what he wanted to hear, and he dropped me off at the Pier Head. The cabbie had gone around the trams that were waiting for the ferry, so I had a short walk to the gangway.

The Overhead Railway rumbled past my head, carrying workers to their dock. The high tide was in, so I had to walk slightly uphill on the gangway to the landing stage. The Mersey looked its same impenetrable self, except that I could see a lot of jellyfish between the landing stage and the sea wall. The Seacombe ferry was coming into view, fog horns blaring, disturbing the gulls and passengers alike. I waited and tried to figure out how this double cross was going to pan out. They would probably just take the photos and not hand over the blade, which was what I expected. But I was ready for all eventualities.

The ferry docked, and the passengers ambled off. It was fairly quiet; rush hour was over. I strolled on and moved up the stairs to the top deck, which was open-air. On the way up, I spotted one shady individual, and sure enough, there was another one standing with Mansell.

I approached them. "Mr Mansell?"

He glared at me and said, "Is that them in the briefcase?"

I nodded. His bodyguard snatched the briefcase out of my hand, and Mansell accompanied him below to check the contents. The other one stared at me and kept his hands in his overcoat pockets. Mansell returned. The briefcase was deposited at my feet.

"I've put your item in the briefcase," Mansell spat out.

I nodded, picked up the briefcase, and was about to move away when Mansell called out, "Not going to check it?"

I looked at him. "I wouldn't know what to check. I'm just following my client's instructions."

"Did that bitch Charlotte put you up to this?"

"Who's Charlotte?"

The two heavyweights started towards me, but Mansell called them off. They went below. I stayed where I was until we reached Seacombe. I watched them depart and saw no dodgy villains get on the ferry for the return trip.

I caught a cab back to the office. The bloody fog was creeping in from the Mersey already. It will be bad tonight. I opened the briefcase, not expecting to find anything. But there was a 10 x 8 print of a naked, statuesque Charlotte kissing and fondling two young, naked oriental girls.

Why did Mansell leave that? I started worrying. He must have realised that he'd been set up and figured, correctly, that Charlotte was actively involved. I needed to think quickly.

I rang Cheapside. The desk sergeant said Detective Shaw was in a meeting but would get him to ring me asap.

I tried to conjure up a working plan but was failing miserably when the phone rang. It was Sugar. "Getting nervous, pal?"

"I must be. Maybe it's a big-night stage fright?"

I heard his chuckle coming down the line: "Don't worry, pal, we've got it covered."

I was still worried. Brilliant! I've got everybody out of town except Charlotte. That could be a big mistake. I must have smoked three or four Passing Clouds before any semblance of an idea popped into my head. I called Binns. "Do you fancy a job tonight?"

"Sure, " came the reply. Where and when?"

I said, "Can you pick me up at about six thirty, and do you have a gun?"

"Yes, is the answer to both questions. See you later."

Chapter 33 Quick and Deadly

I was ready when the car horn sounded—same hat, same coat, but with the Browning in my left-hand pocket.

Outside, Binns was there in a Land Rover, military green with a soft top.

"Sorted?" he asked.

I gave Binns the destination, and while he drove, I brought him up to speed with the handover and the double cross. I told him the photo of Charlotte worried me. That wasn't normal behaviour; that was hatred.

Binns navigated our way through the tunnel and onto Heswall Road. You could hear the wheels humming on the tarmac, the only noise as the encroaching fog got thicker. As we got close to Charlotte's house, a car with its headlights blazing ran us off the road. Binns swerved onto the grass verge and kept us on an even keel.

"What the hell was that?"

Binns muttered, "Some crazy bastard with a death wish."

We drove on, and before we knew it, we were at Charlotte's house. It was visible through the gloom. Binns slowed and stopped just as Geoffrey's Rolls Royce emerged from the driveway. Geoffrey stopped, jumped out, and raced over to us. He was shaking and looked bewildered and terrified at the same time.

"Eneko, two hard-looking bastards dragged Charlotte off in her black Bentley."

"Okay, Geoffrey, just go home. Don't ring anyone, especially the police, and we'll get it sorted."

He stood there speechless, nodded, and went back to his car.

"It must have been those bastards who ran us off the road. They were driving a Bentley," yelled Binns.

He hauled the Land Rover around in a tight circle, and we sped off in pursuit.

"Where to Eneko?"

"Chester."

Binns drove as quickly as he dared. What a pig of a night, but we were about the only cars on the road. After about 20 minutes, we turned onto Welsh Road and headed down to Sealand Road. As we approached the turn, we glimpsed the rear lights of a car in front. But it didn't turn towards Chester; it just carried straight on. We turned on to Sealand Road, but with a howl of brakes, Binns brought the Rover to a halt.

"The rear lights on the car on Welsh Road are from a Bentley."

He reversed and got back onto Welsh Road, but we couldn't see anything. The Land Rover was flying now, all caution to the wind. As we crossed the bridge, the fog thinned, and Binns spotted someone turning right towards Connah's Quay. We followed, but the Bentley had vanished into the fog banks again.

"What the hell is down here?" I yelled over the noise of the engine.

"The River Dee and quicksand."

We slowed down and kept looking, but with visibility down to 10 yards, it was like looking for a needle in a haystack. After a short while, Binns stopped by the river. We both got out and walked along the bank.

Binns issued a warning: "Tread with care. The tide is coming in, and if you get stuck here, you're a goner."

We could have been in a graveyard. Binns grabbed my arm and pointed. Through the fog, we could see the outline of the Bentley starting to take shape.

"Careful, Eneko; those bastards won't be far from the vehicle."

Both of us stood still, not moving a muscle. Sure enough, Binns was right, as we saw two shapes begin to move in the direction of the Bentley.

"Where's Charlotte?" I asked. My voice sounded distant and unreal.

"Gone swimming," one of them growled.

They both produced pistols, but they couldn't see us clearly as we were behind the Bentley. Binns fired four shots. I fired two shots. They fired, but their bullets whistled overhead. I followed Binns as we walked over to them. They were both dead. Binns picked up their guns and put them in his pocket.

We went looking for any sign of Charlotte, but nothing was coming out of that alive.

Binns looked at me. I nodded, and we dragged the bodies over to the quicksand. They sank like stones.

"That's that, Eneko."

"Maybe, but that's Charlotte's Bently, so how did our expired quests get to her house?"

"Good point. You drive the Bentley, and I'll get the Land Rover and head back to her house.

Chapter 34 Geoffrey's Secret

I drove behind Binns. The Bentley's headlights helped, but it was still difficult. Jesus, poor Charlotte, what a way to go. I started to shake with anger. Training took over, and I took some deep breaths. It helped. My ire subsided into cold, calculated fury. We parked in the driveway and took stock. The house looked completely empty. Binns went and checked it out.

"Nobody's home."

My name drifted over from the shadows.

"Eneko, it's me, Geoffrey. I'm at the door."

We walked over to him. Geoffrey was looking worried and deeply unhappy.

"Did you find Charlotte?"

I said, "No, Geoffrey, she's dead. Those two guys you saw killed her."

Geoffrey looked horrified. "Her body," he stammered.

"It will never be found." I stated it coldly. "Geoffrey, just tell me what the hell is going on."

"I was upstairs getting things ready for our little soiree. We meet on Thursdays, as it's the staff's day off. I got to know Charlotte in Hong

Kong, and we hit it off in business and socially. I organised the merchandise in Hong Kong, and she imported it on her company's ships. Mansell knew nothing about it. He would have been furious, and he could have got very violent. I heard the doorbell, and the next thing I knew, those two grabbed Charlotte, pushed her into the back of her Bentley, and roared off."

"Why didn't Charlotte just leave him?"

"Eneko, she did. I think he had some kind of hold on her. She mentioned photographs to me once or twice."

"Geoffrey, why are you still here?"

"Charlotte is a cash-only businesswoman, but she keeps a record of shipments in her safe. She also has some photos of us together with some other girls. And I imagine jewellery, other personal things, and a large amount of cash. I need the shipment records and the photos. The cash is yours. I don't want that bastard Mansell getting his hands on the stuff. He'd ruin me."

"I thought the future was food?"

Geoffrey blanched but said nothing.

I looked at Binns, and he looked at me. I said, "Okay, Geoffrey, we'll get the safe open. You'll get your ledger and photos, but that's it. You were never here; you saw nothing. Is there any reason anyone could associate you with Charlotte—parties, dates, business meetings?"

"No, absolutely nothing."

"Okay, is the car alright there, or does Charlotte park it somewhere else?"

"No, it's fine there. Charlotte just dumps it anywhere."

We followed Geoffrey into an office. There was a large oak desk. The rest of the furniture was a meeting of the west and east in style and colour, pleasant and not overpowering. Geoffrey pointed to a large painting of a schooner. Binns investigated and found the safe behind it. Geoffrey went and stood by the door.

"I'll keep an eye out downstairs. I don't want to see you open the safe or know the combination, either."

Binns peered at the safe. "Twenty minutes," he said.

I waited and checked the rest of the office. Nothing obvious, nothing out of place.

Binns muttered, "It's open."

We looked inside. The ledger was the heavy, old-fashioned type. I took it out. In the corner of the safe was a Manila folder, which was full of photos. Next to the folder was a stack of papers —legal stuff by the look of it.

I called Geoffrey. He came in, looked at the ledger, then the folder, and let out a sigh of relief. I asked what the other papers were. He picked them up, gave them a quick perusal, and said, "Details of her property and bank accounts."

Binns put everything back, locked the safe, and put the picture back securely.

"So that's it, Geoffrey. We were never here."

"Did you get the cash?"

Binns shook his head. "There wasn't any."

Geoffrey looked nonplussed. "That can't be right. We were going to divvy up tonight."

He went over to her desk and opened the drawers. In the top one were two packages of cash. He passed one to each of us.

"I'll leave first. Let's not see each other for a while unless it's an emergency."

I nodded. He left.

Binns and I carefully left everything as it was, turned off the lights, and made sure the front door was locked. We got in the Rover, moved cautiously out onto the main road, and slowly motored back towards Liverpool. Binns drove silently.

"Chester, and tie up the loose ends." He enquired.

"Loose ends?"

"Yeah, remember, the mob from London must have brought a load of cash up with them; there's no way it would fit into the small safe in the lounge. So it could be in the back office."

"True, but the place will be full of cops."

"The house, yes, but not the back office. The law doesn't know it exists."

I whistled, Chester. Here we come.

As we neared Mansell's house, Binns cruised along, taking care to keep as quiet as possible. We parked up two streets away and felt secure in the heavy mist and lack of streetlights. The front of the house was quiet, a police car was out front, one bobby stood outside the front door, the other sat behind the wheel of the car. Binns had brought two ex-army canvas bags that we carried through to the back of the house. He opened a gate that led to a walled garden. Binns fiddled with something hidden in the brickwork and we were in. Once inside the office, Binns opened up the bookcase, and there was the safe. Binns had it open before you could blink. The sword was there where Binns had left it. And next to it, large bundles of cash. I packed them into the canvas bags. It's quite a night's work!

We left as silently as we entered and walked back to the Rover, where Binns loaded the bags. We sat in the Land Rover for a few minutes; there was not a sound to be heard. Binns started the engine, and we moved slowly back to the main road. Binns drove like we were on ice. If anything, the fog was getting thicker. Thankfully, after a nerve-wracking journey, we reached the tunnel. It felt great in the tunnel. You could actually see where you were going.

Binns dropped me off at home. He gave me a hand with the bags, and we dropped them in the office.

"Come round tomorrow, and we'll count tonight's takings."

The Rover slid on the cobbles as it swept up the street. I put on the coffee and poured enough Rémy for three. I put the bundle of cash on the table that Geoffrey had given me and counted it, £12,500 was a lot of cash. God knows how much was in the bags. I picked them all up and dropped them in the gym. I went to bed before I fell over.

Chapter 35 Tying up Loose Ends

In the morning, I put my money in the safe, cleaned my guns, and put them away. Showered and dressed casually in cords and a sweater, I got rid of the clutter in the office and readied my coffee maker. The doorbell rang, and I opened up to Sugar's beaming smile. He slapped me on the shoulder.

"I'm hiring you as my agent. My super thinks I'm the reincarnation of Sherlock Holmes."

I laughed and poured the coffee. "So, what happened?"

"Eneko, settle yourself down. This story is going to take a while to spin. I took your advice and let the gang pick up the drugs at the docks. The fog was awful, but the lads did a great job of tailing the two cars to the tunnel. We were waiting on the Birkenhead side for the cars when one of my lads noticed another car parked just up from the tunnel. It was one of the cars in those photos, so we hung back, informed my mate in Chester, and he had an unmarked car pick them up as they passed the zoo."

"Two of the cars were parked near Mansell's place, a third drifted up alongside them, and stuff was transferred into the boot. One geezer stayed in the car, and the others went into the house. Two Cheshire bobbies sidled up to the motor and had our cockney friend bound and gagged before he knew what hit him."

"My mate had the search warrant for harbouring a convicted felon. He also placed armed men at the side of the house. I knocked on the door, and when Mansell came to the door, I asked him if he knew one of his guests was a convicted felon. He tried slamming the door shut, but my size 13 boots put an end to that. Four more of them came rushing to help Mansell, but six of our lads smashed the door open. The guy we had a warrant for pulled a gun, but when he saw our arsenal, he dropped it like a hot potato. Mansell was screaming blue murder, demanding a lawyer, and the boys from the smoke were trying to brazen it out. But having a firearm is a no no. Two of the others were armed as well."

"They were all frogmarched out. My inspector mate had opened the boot: 50 lbs of heroin, 25 lbs of morphine, amphetamines, and some other unnamed drugs. And for good measure, five pistols and some folding money— an Aladdin's cave of goodies."

"Any repercussions?"

"Are you kidding! Some of those photos contained some of the so-called cream of society: lawyers, politicians, well known gangsters, and a couple of people in the movie business. The Chief Superintendent has already been on and asked me if I did everything by the book."

"At 6 am, Mansell's lawyers turned up demanding entry to his property to secure his business interests. It's a lawyer's wet dream, mate."

I poured another couple of Rémys and topped up the coffee. "If this was tea, the leaves would predict promotion, Mr Shaw."

Sugar laughed. "Any news on the protection racket?"

"It's all gone a bit, quiet Sugar; I'll let you know."

He stood up; I could swear he'd grown. He slapped me on the shoulder again.

"Got to go. Tickets for the match with the big cheese."

Chapter 36 Counting the Take

The phone rang. "Is it safe to come around?"

"Yeah, the law has left."

Binns came in. I shut the door and showed him through to my apartment.

"Take a seat. I'll get the night's takings."

I went down to the cellar, opened the safe, grabbed the bags, brought them into the lounge, and tipped the money out.

"Jesus," whispered Binns. "I thought the £12,500 from Geoffrey was a wedge, but this," his voice tailed off.

The count was simple enough. The notes were in bundles of £1000. There were two hundred fivers in each bundle. There were 100 bundles, exactly.

"I'd pay a lot to see Mansell's face when they realise the money has gone."

Binns laughed. "I'd like to see the faces on the cockney mob. Big cockup losing all that dope."

I started packing Binns's share into the canvas bag. "Any plans for the money?"

"Yeah, but nothing daft. I've got a cottage up on the Welsh hills. It's got a barn attached that

I'm not using. My nearest neighbours are over the hill down in the valley, about two miles away, and I know they're struggling. There's three families there, good people; most of the menfolk were killed during the war, so life's tough. I'm planning to invest in livestock: some more sheep —and let them use the barn, manage the livestock, and run the business. I'll just be a silent partner. I've also got my old army pal, Rabbit. He's excellent with livestock, horses, and ponies. And reliable as clockwork, as long as I keep him from being broke. But give him a wedge, and he'd be the talk of the valleys."

Binns looked at me, and I said, "No, nothing at the moment. I'll think about it. But remember, we've got business Tuesday evening. Bring a weapon."

"Okay, here about 5 pm?"

I nodded. He grinned, picked up his bag, winked, and sauntered off.

Chapter 37 Holidays for Some

I put all my hard earned cash back in the safe. I realised I was starving. The fridge revealed bacon, sausages, and eggs—a winning combination. After brunch, I decided a pint was in order. I had my coat and scarf on when the phone rang. It was George.

"I thought I said, " Call me next week when it's safe."

"Eneko, just because you refuse to read the newspapers doesn't mean there's no news. The Chester raid is all over the headlines. And Bee wants to ring Kimi in New York."

I tried to say something, but George beat me to it. "And don't you bloody move. We'll be there in 10 minutes."

The office door opened with a crash. The girls had arrived. George kissed me full on the lips. Begonia hugged me and kissed me on both cheeks. They looked full of it. George had the coffee going in a flash. Begonia turned server and poured the Rémy. I sat down.

George opened the newspaper: "The boys in blue pulled off a daring raid and captured an armed guy on the run, loads of illegal drugs, and various weapons. Your mate, Sugar, is turning into the public's crime busting hero, according to the papers."

"They like tall cops; it makes them feel safe."

Begonia smiled. "I like my heroes—shorter, slimmer, and with a good fashion sense."

George pretended to puke, and Begonia laughed. "He's your boss."

I sat down and gathered my thoughts. What to tell them and what to skip.

"Girls, I'll bring you up to date. What you read in the papers is the truth, more or less. It looks like Mansell and his cronies are going to have a hard time getting out of this one. They also found incriminating photos of child pornography with well-known people, which will never see the light of day. And guns and drugs are bad medicine, so I think we can say goodbye to them for a good while."

"Good riddance," George spat out.

"I will not be busy this week and next, so why don't you and Begonia go on a holiday?"

They both laughed. "I think it's called money."

I smiled and pulled two envelopes from my briefcase. One was the envelope Begonia had given me to cover the cost of my investigation, which I handed back to her.

"No fee is required, Begonia. It was a pleasure, and my reputation has increased in value by much more."

"Thank you, Eneko."

I handed George the other envelope — "A bonus for putting up with me."

George hugged me.

"Are you girls going to Spain?"

Begonia nodded. "Yeah, but not for a few days. George needs to tie up some details in Wales."

"I've got a date with a pint in the White Star in two minutes. Call me when you can. And use the phone to call Kimiko and give both of them my best."

"Oh," Begonia said, "Kimiko said you need to get out more. She's worried about you. After the night of photographing with you, she said Kaimana was like a rampant bull, yet you went home and drank coffee."

I was lost for words.

They laughed, I got more hugs and kisses, and they were gone. The White Star was empty. Everyone was at the match. I looked over at Masie. The pint was already in her hand.

"Ta, Masie."

"How's your sister?"

"She's struggling, but her heart is in the right place. She'll come good. But that pimp's a right one. He'd sell his own mother for a quid."

"Is he still giving her a hard time?"

"Yeah, I'm getting worried. She came around to see me and wanted to pass on her apologies to you. The pimp and his mates were laughing and saying they'd sorted you out."

"Have you got their names?"

149

Maisy smiled and got a pencil from the till and wrote three names on the back of a piece of the till roll. "Not me that gave you the names, Eneko."

I tapped my nose with my forefinger and went back to my pint.

Chapter 38 Boys with Guns

The morning started well enough; the coffee and toast hit the spot.

The phone rang; its jarring woke me from my revelry. It was Bernie Goldstein, the jeweller.

"All hell's broken out. Three jewellers got threatened last night, and two of them got duffed over."

"Jesus! What's with these guys? Don't they like talking?"

"They want a meeting today at my shop at 6 pm. Can you make it?"

"Sure, I'll be there."

This problem with the jewellers needed to be put to bed soon. The Chester case had been time-consuming. Boys with guns, eh? This could end in only one way.

I called Binns. "I need a hand tonight, pal. Are you up for it?"

"No problem. Where and when?"

"The meeting with the jewel merchants is at Bernie's place on Bold Street at 6 pm. I'll see what they want. If you could follow the yobs and try to get their exact location, that would be a great help. It's not expected to be too foggy tonight, so trailing them should be routine, but be careful. These cowboys are packing."

I went through my usual routine and cleaned my weapons in case I needed them. The phone rang a few times with just inquiries, nothing of earth-shattering importance but business. I told them all I'd be in touch next week.

Around 5 pm, I made a coffee and got my gear ready: black cords, a sweater, and a black overcoat with big pockets on the side, large enough to take a Browning and a Beretta.

I walked to Bernie's place and arrived at 5:50 pm. The shop was closed, but he was waiting and opened the door. He showed me through to the back of the shop. Five elderly merchants were standing there, looking worried. A sixth guy stood out as he looked about 35, slim, and athletic.

Bernie introduced me to the group. I was just about to explain my role when someone hammered on the front door. Bernie hurried to open it, and the rest of the group, apart from the young guy, looked even more nervous. Four yobs strolled in as if they owned the place, swore at Bernie, and barged into the back office. They stood by the door. I was to the left, and the merchants were standing behind the desk.

"So which one of youse is the mouthpiece?"

I looked at them. "You're looking at him, pal."

"So the Jew boys have got a Chinese nancy boy doing their dirty work, eh?"

I hit him with a roundhouse kick to the jaw. He hit the floor like a sack of cement. That stopped the others in their tracks.

I threw my business card at one of them. "When you can dig someone up with half a brain, call me; until then, pick up that piece of crap and piss off."

They picked up their mate, who was still looking second-best. One of them said, "You'll be hearing from us, pal."

"That's the general idea, mate."

The shop door slammed. Bernie looked at me and said, "Eneko, was that the right thing to do?"

"Bernie, I don't take racist crap from anyone. Don't worry, I'll get it sorted this week."

The other merchants mumbled their thanks, but they all looked concerned. I smiled and made my way to the shop door. I stopped on the pavement and looked to see if any of the low life was hanging about when a voice behind me said, "Nice work, Mr Sora."

I turned, and the young, athletic merchant stood there with his hand out. I shook it, and he popped a business card into my hand. I looked at it, Jacob Cardozo.

Jacob said, "If you need any help, please ask. I have experience in these matters."

"I'm sure I'll be calling you."

He grinned. "I'll be waiting."

Chapter 39 Binn's Recce

I wandered back to the office. Binns would drop by rather than call. Sure enough, at 9 pm, the office doorbell rang.

Binns entered, looking his usual unflappable self.

"Any problems?"

"No, they were easy to follow. One of them looked groggy, though."

"The one with the mouth made a crack about Bernie and me. He deserved a smack in the mouth—an easy target. How about your end?"

"I followed them to Sefton Park, where they entered a driveway to one of those old houses. I gave them a while to get settled and then slipped up the driveway. On the front door is a brass plate with Gisburn Import and Export written on it. The house has a lounge at the back with French windows that open out onto a patio and a well-kept garden. From the shadows, I had a clear view of the lounge. There were eight of them in there: the idiots that went to the meeting, plus two older, heavy men and a very well-kept woman of about fifty. She was doing most of the talking, and the heavies were doing most of the listening. I was too far away to catch what they were saying, but I got some photos of them, plus all the vehicle registrations."

"I'll develop them in the morning. What do you reckon, all brawn and no brain?"

"I'd say the ones doing the talking look like they have a brain, but we'll see. We could get inside sometime this week. In the meantime, let's try to put names on faces and check Companies House about their business."

"Okay, can you check out Companies House, and I'll get Sugar to check out some mugshots?"

We agreed to meet in 48 hours or sooner if the brains of the organisation got back to me. Binns left, and I grabbed a sandwich and hit the sack.

Chapter 40 Mugs and Mug Shots

In the morning, I gave Sugar a bell. I told him I'd got some mug shots and I could do with putting a name to a face. He said he'd pop around for lunch. I developed the stuff and got the table prepared. At 11:30 am, Sugar opened the office door. I motioned for him to come over to the table and laid out the photos. He looked at them and held up a photo of the woman and another one of an older, well-dressed guy with white bushy hair.

"This guy got out about 6 months ago, nasty bastard. Old school used to hang around with your old mates, the Randall brothers. The other older guy doesn't ring any bells, but the woman does. She was married to Giacometti Pasolini, an Italian fascist who, last we heard, was back in Turin. The young bloods are local scum, not a brain between them, but nasty."

"Do they have a big protection racket going, or are they just starting?"

"We have heard rumours, but you know what people are like. They keep it close to the chests, especially if family members are a target."

I let that one hang for a moment. I could be alone with this one, I thought.

"Fancy a pint?"

Sugar lipped his lips and grinned. I shut the office, and we set off. Last night's rain had cleaned things up, and even the air smelled fresher. The White Star had only just opened; just a couple of coopers were in, supping pints of Bass and smoking woodbines. They were lip-reading each other, as all coopers are as deaf as posts.

"Now that's a skill—I should put all my junior constables on a course."

I laughed. "The criminal class would be up in arms."

I passed Sugar the piece of paper Masie had given me. "Ring any bells?"

He looked the names over and said, "One of them rings a bell, pimp, I think. Just low-life living off a few bints, problem?"

"No, nothing to worry about."

After Sugar left, I went back to the office. It seemed out of balance without George. I sat at her desk and wondered what this protection racket was all about. 1930s Chicago-style protection with guns. It didn't sound like a winner to me. There had to be another reason for the in-your-face threats of violence. I went through the names of the local mobsters and came up with nothing. The lady could be another story, as could the mystery man. We needed to find the connection.

The doorbell rang, and in walked Jacob Cardozo. I told him to take a seat.

"I'm just making coffee. Would you like one?" He accepted with a smile and a nod. I brought the coffee back to the table. He stirred in two sugars and tried it.

"Excellent coffee. I see you use an Italian coffee maker."

"The best."

"Mr Sora."

"Please call me Eneko, Jacob."

"Okay, Eneko, I need to tell you the real reason I am here in Liverpool. I am an Italian Jew. I fought against the SS and the Italian fascists. Since the end of WW11, I have spent my time assisting Jewish refugees to get to Israel. All over Europe, Jewish organisations in cities and towns raise money for this purpose. Since '52, we have had problems with so-called protection rackets springing up all over the place. The idea is to stop Jewish organisations from raising money. While simultaneously using violence against them, just like here in Liverpool."

"I didn't realise it was that coordinated."

"The thugs that came to the meeting are just muscle, but behind them is a fascist group with its chief headquarters in Italy."

"Are Giacometti Pasolini and his English wife involved in this racket?"

"Yes, she is called Susanna, a real fascist. But the other older guy is an Italian, Alberto Ricci. A fascist of the old school and a real Jew hater. If you remember the atrocities in Piedmont, you can understand what kind of man he is."

"Do you have a plan?"

"I do. I'm going to grab him, put him on a ship, and transport him to Italy. He's a wanted criminal there for many crimes, so they will convict him for sure."

"Do you need a hand?"

"Yes, I do; I'm short on manpower. My plan is to kidnap him and drive him to the docks. I'm on my own in England, but I have colleagues onboard the ship."

"Let's meet here tomorrow at six, unless I hear anything different. I'll bring a friend who's very well acquainted with this sort of work."

"Excellent, Eneko; tomorrow it is."

Chapter 41 Scuffle in Sefton Park

Binns rang later. I told him we were going to meet up tomorrow with Joseph Cardoza at 6 pm and do a bit of illegal exercise, but with good on our side.

"It's always good to do good. Their company is just a front for moving freight around, but there doesn't seem to be much of it. "

I put the phone down. We needed to be on the ball. These local villains came across as dangerous idiots.

The phone rang. Sugar's laughter came down the line like a breath of fresh air: "It's all kicked off, lawyers accusing the police of theft of personal property, but not saying what. At first, bail was refused for Mansell, but that was overturned, and he posted bail at £15,000. He wasn't happy, nor were the boys from the smoke who were refused."

"Where's he staying on bail?"

"At his gaff in Chester. No sooner had he got there, the telephone lines went into overdrive, screams of outrage from him, lawyers sputtering, but when asked about what, silence. The story going around is that his wife, Charlotte, has disappeared with his money, which he doesn't want to tell us about. Absolutely hilarious! Catch up later, Eneko, when I stop laughing."

Interesting. Could Binns and I be in the clear? That could be a result. The rest of the day I spent answering the phone; nothing was urgent. It could all wait until next week. I checked my weapons, cleaned them, and loaded them, ready for action. That was followed by a couple of hours of practising Kendo and doing some katas. After an early tea, I was ready for the evening's entertainment.

Jacob arrived first, carrying a holdall, quickly followed by Binns. I introduced them to each other, and we got down to the plan.

Jacob spoke first. "I really appreciate your help, but if it turns violent tonight, please leave it to me. I have some rope and gags in the bag, and I will take Susanna as well. She has crimes to answer for in Italy."

I placed my guns on the table. Binns did the same. Jacob whistled and put a Beretta down. We all smiled.

"We'll follow your lead, Jacob, but don't worry. We know how to use these weapons. You follow us in your car. Binns and I will park up outside the house and do a recce. I think it's best if we keep the vehicles on the road. The fog is still around and probably going to get a lot worse, which should give us the cover we need."

Binns and I climbed into the Rover, with Jacob behind in a black Rover. We entered the park and circled it until we got close to the gang's house. We parked up and waited for Jacob. The house was shrouded in fog, and with the trees and the lack of street lights, it was unlikely we'd be spotted. Binns went for his recce and came back after about 15 minutes.

"The Italian guy is on the phone, talking in Italian. The woman is with him. Two of the young villains are in the next room listening to music and playing snooker; there is no sign of the others."

"Okay, Jacob, I'll take the boys in the snooker room; you take your two, and I'll come and help when I've dealt with mine. Binns, you play back up, and if the others arrive, let us know."

"Okay, no problem. I've opened the back door, so all you need to do is push it. The two you want, Jacob, are in the room on your right as you enter. You'll be able to hear them talking. Eneko, your two are in the room further up on your left; you'll hear the music. I'll give you five minutes, then I'll drive the Rover in, and I suggest that both of you get the luggage to the docks. I'll stay behind and make sure we're in the clear."

Jacob and I nodded. We set off around the house to the back door. Jacob pushed the door gently. We moved inside, and at once we could hear voices speaking excitedly in Italian. Jacob put his hand on my shoulder and pointed to my door. I pushed open the snooker room door. The two young thugs had snooker cues in hand and were wearing shoulder holsters, like in the old gangster movies. We looked at each other, and before a word was said, they went for their guns. I shot them both, the noise echoing off the walls.

I heard rumblings from the back room. I ran out, and Jacob had got them both tied and gagged. He raised an eyebrow at me. I shook my head.

We heard wheels on the gravel. Binns was there. We loaded the two into the back.

Binns said, "Did I hear shots?"

"Yes, it couldn't be helped. Gun happy idiots."

Binns said, "Go, I'll sort this out."

Jacob drove. The two in the back were staring daggers at me. Jacob drove into the Huskisson dock and stopped alongside a small freighter. As soon as we parked, five men were by the side of the car. The air was filled with Italian expletives. Jacob gave his orders, and the crew went aboard with two extra passengers.

We drove back to the office. The fog was getting bad again. At the office, I made coffee and opened a new bottle of Rémy. We heard the Rover slide on the cobbles and stop. Binns came in and smiled.

"That was close. After you left, I went into the house to make sure you two hadn't left anything behind. I was just about to leave when I heard a car on the gravel. I stepped back into the snooker room. There were shouts, but I couldn't hear what was being said when the old bloke and the two young gunmen came charging in. I shot first. They didn't have a chance. They were all dead—five bodies in all. I closed all the doors and then emptied the weapons into whichever body was handy. I put some bullets in the walls and furniture to make it look like a shootout at the OK Corral. Let the cops sort that one out, eh?"

Binns took a big gulp of his Rémy.

Jacob said, "That was quick thinking, Binns. I think you have tidied up all the loose ends."

"I wonder what the law will make of that," I said.

"No doubt your mate, Sugar, will let us know."

"Gentlemen, thank you so much. I'll be on my way. If you are ever in Italy, you have my card; I'm forever in your debt. And don't worry about Bernie and the other merchants. I will make a very plausible excuse."

We said our goodbyes, and Binns and I sat down for a quiet smoke and a drink.

"Eneko, we're becoming trigger happy, mate. Now what?"

"Let's get some shut-eye. I've got a feeling Sugar is going to be on his way around tomorrow morning."

Binns grinned and left. He was so cool, nothing fazed him. What a partner in crime! I cleaned up, put the weapons away, and hit the sack.

Chapter 42 The Day after the Night before

The doorbell rang. So I finished dressing and hurried to answer the office door. It was Sugar.

"A little late, aren't you, mate?"

"Yeah, George is away for a few days, so I can have a lie-in. I'll put the coffee on."

He threw a bag of scones over. I buttered some and added some of George's blackcurrant jam.

"So what's the news with the London mob and our mate, Mansell?"

"Oh, he's off the front page, new competition mate."

"Who?"

"George is right. You don't listen to the news, do you?"

"It's all the same old waffle. Don't you remember I used to write some of it?"

"Well, this is big news for Liverpool. According to the Post, Last night there was a major shootout between known hoodlums in the Sefton Park area of the city."

"Hoodlums, are we going all 1920s Chicago?"

"Yeah, that fella you showed me a photo of, the ex-Randall gang member, was involved in a shootout. Five killed in total!"

"What, in Liverpool?"

"Yeah, in good old Liverpool."

"Well, who knocked them off?"

"It appears they knocked each other off; five weapons were recovered, all empty, bullets in bodies, walls, and furniture. However, we found bullets from another two weapons not found at the scene, and the woman and the other guy have disappeared."

"Weird. They were the only ones to get out alive."

"Yeah, I couldn't care less, but the boss doesn't like loose ends. The other news is that Mansell is lying low; his missus is nowhere to be found."

We talked football while munching away on scones and drinking coffee. The phone rang. It was for Sugar. I passed the phone over.

"Okay, 10 minutes. Got to go, mate. Things are coming to the boil."

I sat down and wrote it all down: protection racket, done and dusted; shoot out to remain a mystery; Charlotte likewise. But what about her assailants? Haven't they been missed? And if they have, what?

The phone rang. Binns said, "I'm in the phone box around the corner. I've been at the top of your street for the last hour. One of those motors we spotted is just up from your office with two of Mansell's men in it."

Jesus, I didn't think Mansell had any more heavies left.

"If you think about it, you're the only one that might have any ideas about what went down. Just sit tight. I'll stay here, and when they call on you, I'll be handy."

"Okay."

I made myself a coffee, lit another cigarette, and waited. Sure enough, after about 15 minutes, the office door was almost knocked off its hinges as two of Mansell's heavies arrived. One I recognised from the drop.

"Good morning, Can I help you? "

"We want to talk to your client, the guy who wanted the sword."

I took a drag of my cigarette and said, "Not possible, client confidentiality, and also, he's out of the country."

He picked up the phone and dialled. It was answered. He handed me the phone.

Mansell came on the line, "I think you know what's going on, Mr Sora. I'm getting the sword valued today, and if your client wants it, the price has just gone up. I'd also like to talk to Begonia and Kimiko today."

"Kimiko has left the country, and Begonia is out of town this week."

"And your secretary, is she out of town in Wales, perhaps?"

"I didn't ask."

"I'll call you tomorrow, and we can talk about prices."

I handed the phone over, the heavy muttered something, and put the phone down. They walked out.

Two minutes later, the door opened and Binns walked in.

"The heavies have just driven off, mate."

I explained what had happened and how the conversation went. Binns looked anxious. "We need to get in touch with George."

"How?"

"Where is she staying?"

"I told him."

"Okay, no problem." He picked up the phone. It rang a few times, and then somebody answered.

"It's Binns here; Is Rabbit about? Okay, put him on." He spoke in Welsh for about five minutes. Then he explained what he said to Rabbit.

"Do you think George will go for that?"

"No problem; her family and Rabbit's go way back."

"How long will it take the girls to get to the pub?"

"An hour."

"Then what?"

"Don't worry, it'll be right."

We sat and drank coffee for about an hour and a half. Then the phone rang. I grabbed it.

"Rabbit here."

169

"I'm putting Binns on."

Binns said, "Yeah, what? Okay, Rabbit, calm down. Where did they go? Yeah, I know it; it's all good. Now listen, Rabbit, drive to their place, but park the car somewhere I can spot it. Keep your car ready, and when we come out with the girls, you drive to my place above Bylchau. In the cottage there's all the essentials, plus wine, brandy, and a shotgun."

"What the hell's happening, Binns?"

"Mansell's heavies grabbed them from George's place. They've gone up to a house I know in one of the more secluded valleys, owned by Charlotte. He said the heavies didn't see him as they drove out, but he spotted them."

"Thank God! Okay, I've been thinking Mansell is a dummy, but when he knows the sword is worth peanuts, he's going to put two and two together. I doubt if Charlotte knew the combination to his safe, so he's going to make some inquiries and figure that the sword and the money go together. Mansell must have figured out that George is the possible missing link."

Binns took off to get his Land Rover, and I got my guns and ammo, grabbed a parka, gloves, and a woolly hat, and walked down to meet Binns.

Chapter 43 Military Manoeuvres

Binns drove, stopped, and turned the lights off, but nothing came past us. He then shot off like a bolt out of the blue and nipped down a few back alleys before entering the tunnel.

"Eneko, keep your eyes peeled. You're looking for a black Rover 75 with that number plate. He handed me a piece of paper. They may have another car waiting on the other side of the tunnel, so anything suspicious, sing out."

I kept my eyes on the road behind me, but I saw nothing. As we emerged on the Birkenhead side, the fog had already drifted in. We were in for a long, old drive. Binns drove on, and we kept our own thoughts to ourselves.

"We're just entering God's country. Another hour should do it."

The fog was patchy; Binns carried on, but quicker. After forty minutes, he stopped.

"Eneko, open that gate, and I can put the Land Rover there out of sight."

I opened the gate, and Binns stopped behind a stone wall that hid it. I grabbed my pack, and Binns did the same. Binns had his compass and a map. He spent a few minutes checking his bearings, then pointed, and I followed. The higher we went, the more sleet dropped, leaving a track behind us.

"Don't worry about our tracks. The snow will soon fill them in."

Once Binns had navigated us to the top, we dropped onto a decent dirt road. Someone whistled as he came out of the shadows. It was Rabbit. We nodded at each other, and he pointed up the slope. We could see a group of cottages and barns. In the front, near a wall, were two parked cars.

Binns said, "I'll do a recce. I know the area. You two stay here and keep calm."

I nodded. Binns worked his way down to the tree line, then hugged the wall until he got to one cottage. Then he was out of sight for a good 15 minutes. Blacker than pitch, with hill fog rolling down the valley walls, I wondered how Binns could see anything. I heard a slight foot movement, and next thing Binns was at my side.

"There are people in three of the cottages. George and Begonia are in the farthest one to our left, with two or three men. The middle cottage has two others, and the cottage nearest us has two more. Rabbit, stay here, and when the girls arrive, you take off with them, okay?"

"Got it."

Binns moved forward, and I followed. We reached the wall, stopped, and waited.

"They're getting ready to eat. You take the cottage with the girls. Someone will have to deliver the food to the villains in the cottage. Take him out, and then you're on your own. I may shoot the lot, so if you hear shots, don't worry, just do your job."

I nodded, and we waited. There were some muted voices and the crunch of footsteps as someone was moving. Binns tapped me on the shoulder and pointed to a shape making its way to the last cottage. I moved over the ground and got to the cottage as he delivered the food. I heard some mumbling and a laugh. The door closed, and Mansell's man was within my reach. I hit him over the head with my pistol butt. He didn't make a sound. I rolled him into the shrubbery. I tapped on the door, and someone opened it. I smashed him in the face. Blood splattered everywhere. He collapsed to the floor, and to make sure he stayed there, I kicked him in the head.

George and Begonia were both naked on tiptoes, with their hands tied behind them and secured by rope hanging from the rafters. George had a black eye and weals across her buttocks, blood rolling down her chin. Begonia looked in much the same condition, but she was unconscious.

"Nice of you to stop by; you can watch the fun," said a tall, red-headed, muscle-bound idiot holding an axe handle. Next to him was his doppelganger, holding another axe handle.

I was going to enjoy this. These two idiots didn't have a clue what was going to hit them. The two of them spread out. I kept moving to my left. Redhead attacked like a baseball player going for a home run. I stepped inside his swing, shouldered the axe shaft and him at the same time while gripping his right arm, which I bent over my left shoulder, smashing him into the floor, giving him a shattered shoulder and a face full of broken teeth. The other heavy attacked with a similar action, but by now I had his mate's axe handle in my hands. I countered, broke his right arm, and then knocked him senseless with a chopping swing to his temple. The silence was deafening. I lifted George down. She was weeping but more concerned about Begonia, who was still unconscious.

"George, get dressed and get some clothes on Begonia. I'll be back in a minute."

George nodded, and as I opened the door, I heard gunshots. I raced over to the next cottage. Binns came flying out, returning fire as he dove for the trees. Two gunmen came running out. I opened up with both pistols. They were dead before they hit the floor.

"Eneko, that's the lot. I shot the rest of them."

"Come on, let's get the girls. They're a mess."

George had got some clothes on Begonia and had dressed herself, but she looked in shock. Begonia was still out. Binns looked at me.

"What now?"

"Let's get them to Rabbit's car and up to your place and get them fixed up."

Binns picked up Begonia, and I put my arms around George and helped her to the car. Rabbit was in the car, ready to go.

"Rabbit, watch out for other villains and help them clean up and get some coffee and brandy inside them. We'll see you soon."

Rabbit waved, and he was gone. We went back to the cottage where the girls had been. We heard sounds of life inside and outside the cottage, but Binns shot them all without a word.

"So, Eneko, we have a choice: burn the place down or drag the bodies out and into the cars and dump them with their mates in Connah's Quay."

"Let's dump them with their mates. It would be a pity to burn this place down."

"Okay, I'll get Rabbit to clean this place up. It'll look as good as new."

"Now what?"

"Put the bodies in the cars. First stop, Connah's Quay. Whatever you do, don't get stopped by the law."

We got our gear out, put it in the boot, and pushed the bodies into the back of the cars, covering them with blankets.

Binns said, "With a bit of luck, we should get to Connah's Quay about midnight. We'll be invisible."

I worked my way down the lane and onto the main road. Binns drove past me, so I followed. We didn't see anyone, not even when we approached Connah's Quay. The fog felt impenetrable and claustrophobic. We drove the cars up the track and emptied the cargo into the quicksand. The bodies sank without a murmur.

"Eneko, let's finish this tonight. We can drop off their car right near Mansell's place. The law doesn't like messy cars with bloodstains."

Chapter 44 Time to Go

We drove in a convoy to Chester. I parked about three streets away from the house. Binns parked just around the corner from Mansell's place. I followed Binns. He went to the back of the house and let us in via the side door. As we listened, we could hear an argument coming from the study. Mansell was saying someone was getting the information from the secretary. A real, cockney voice started speaking.

"Mansell, why would the girl know anything? You're having a laugh, matey. The law got the dope, the money's gone, the sword is worth diddly squat, and you're blaming the secretary."

"Bobby, shoot him."

Mansell didn't have time to say a word before two shots rang out.

Binns looked at me. I nodded.

The cockney voice spoke again: "I hate coming up north, especially when it costs me money. Harry, get the motor. Let's get the feck out of here."

The door opened, and Binns and I opened fire. The three of them hit the floor, dead as...

"Binns said, "It doesn't sound like there's anyone out front, but we'll go out the back. Let the Chester constabulary sort this out."

We walked out of the back of the house. All was silent. There didn't appear to be any other cars with London gangsters, so we got in the car, and Binns said, "I'll get Rabbit to dump this car later, somewhere handy like the bottom of a quarry."

We headed back to God's country.

Chapter 45 Time to Digest

We arrived at his place about 5 am. Rabbit was at the door, shotgun in hand.

"Top job, me old mate, got one last job for you. Dump this car somewhere; no one will find it. And then the big place needs cleaning up. Can you manage on your own?"

"Yeah, I'll get what I need from my place. Begonia is still out, and George is in shock, but I think she's more worried about Begonia."

Rabbit got in the car and drove off. Binns got our gear out of the boot. In the cottage, Binns went into the back, and soon after, I heard a boiler start up. George was on the settee, shaking. She grabbed my arms and wrapped them around herself. It took a while, but she finally drifted off to sleep.

"Eneko, Begonia's got a real smack on the back of her head, and they have hammered her around her shoulders and all over, I expect, but I haven't checked."

"Let's leave them be, and then in the morning we can check the damage and get some medical help. I don't know about you, Binns, but the coffee smells good, and the brandy looks even better."

"Binns, I've just had an idea. George has a friend, Rhian, the vet. Do you reckon she could help?"

"Rhian, that sounds like a plan. I know her. I'll let you sort the bathing out, and I'll pick up my car and see Rhian."

Binns left, and I tried to revive the girls. George was moving, so I helped her up and moved her to the bathroom. The bathroom was all black-and-white tiles with a very large tub. I explained to George that a bath would help with the bruising; she gripped me as I helped her into the bath and let her soak. After about twenty minutes, she said, "Where's Bee?"

"She's still dead to the world. When you get out of the tub, I'm going to put her in and try to ease her bruising."

"Okay, boss." She stood up, and I helped her out of the bath.

"If you keep seeing me naked much more, you'll have to marry me."

I smiled and helped her back to bed. Begonia was fretting in her sleep. George gave her a hug, and Begonia woke up. She grabbed George and started sobbing and embracing her.

Begonia looked at me, smiled, and said, "Where am I?"

I picked her up and helped her into the bathroom. She had welts around her buttocks, her thighs, and her breasts. She'd also taken some hard blows to the head. I helped her into the tub. She was in pain, but she relaxed. I added some more hot water, shampooed her hair, and let her soak. After 20 minutes, I got her out of the bath, towelled her down, and put her to bed with George. George smiled; they clung to each other and drifted off.

I made some more coffee, drank another Rémy or two, smoked a few more Passing Clouds, and twiddled my thumbs. I heard the Land Rover before I saw anything. Binns came in with Rhian; they were both carrying bags. Binns had a bag full of groceries, and Rhian had her vet's bag.

Rhian woke the girls and told us to go into the kitchen and make breakfast. We could hear her talking to the girls. Rhian called me, and I went back into the living room. George was lying naked on the covers. Rhian had her medical bag equipment open.

"While I look at Begonia, turn George on her front and use this ointment on her bruises. Make sure you spread the stuff all over."

I turned George over and started working the ointment into her bruises. Her buttocks were red and raw, and she had scratches and bruises down her legs. The small of her back was black with a nasty-looking welt. I could see Rhian working the ointment into Begonia's breasts and stomach and inspecting her face and jawline. We worked for about 20 minutes. Then Rhian nodded to the kitchen. I went in, and I could smell the bacon cooking.

Rhian came into the kitchen, took a swig of Rémy, and sat down with a coffee cup in her hand.

"Those girls look like they've gone ten rounds with Don Cockell. The bastards who did that better be in the hospital or jail. And what the hell are you doing by letting them get stuck in that kind of situation?"

That last remark was spat at me. Before I could utter a word, she said, "I've given them a sedative, strong enough to knock a horse over. They'll sleep until tomorrow morning, and when they wake up, they'll be stiff and sore. The bath is an excellent idea and will help. I'll come back tomorrow around lunchtime, and they'll come and stay with me so I can help them get back on their feet."

I was about to say something, but the look I got stopped me in my tracks.

"Eneko, are you sure there are no more of these animals out there that could turn up and do this again?"

"No, that gang is all washed up."

Binns said, "I'll get the Rover."

Rhian lent her head towards me, kissed me, grabbed my balls, and squeezed.

"Make sure there is no more scum out there looking for the girls—remember, I'm a vet."

I spent the day watching the girls. Binns returned at 6 p.m., and we cooked up a couple of steaks, drank some red wine, and finished it with coffee and Rémy. The girls didn't move a muscle, even during the night. Rhian arrived at 10 am and woke the girls. She got the girls in the bathroom one at a time, checked for blood in their urine, and gave them a thorough examination. She'd brought pyjamas, slippers, and big parkas. The girls drank some coffee, and a little Rémy and Rhian got them ready to go. Binns said the mist was just around the hilltops, and it wouldn't slow them down. George put her arms around Binns and kissed him on both cheeks. Begonia kissed me and whispered her thanks in Basque. Binns helped Begonia to the Rover, and George put her arms around me, kissing me with genuine passion on my lips. I was getting far too aroused. Rhian got George by the arm, out of the door, and into the Rover. Binns tooted the horn.

"See you in an hour."

Binns and I stayed the night and talked things through. We agreed it had turned out very well for us, as long as the Cheshire Police didn't start getting nosy. Binns dropped me off at the office and said he would pop by maybe later today or tomorrow. I said I'd be in the office all day as I'd got things to do.

After a hot bath, I felt less depressed. I changed, cleaned my guns, and put them away. Time for a pint, I thought. As I was walking up the s treet, trying to make things out in the fog, my name rumbled through the murk. I turned, and Sugar was right behind me.

"Alright, Sugar, you lost again?"

"No, I thought it was time I bought you a pint and chewed the fat."

The landlord was behind the bar. He pulled us a couple of pints, gave Sugar a fellow professional nod, and disappeared back into the cellar.

Sugar said, "Did you catch the news this morning?"

"What news?"

"You live in your own world, mate; you really do. Headlines: A prominent Chester business executive was shot to death in his own house by unknown assailants. Three more bodies were found at the same location; police have no further details. The sordid details: Mansell got hit with two shots, and the other three villains got shot with two rounds each as well. One top man and two bits of muscle from the smoke, a result, as they say."

"Those Londoners should stay on their own patch."

"Scotland Yard is sending up some of their blokes to help with forensics, fingerprints, etc. They don't like their cockney villains getting shot outside the smoke. A bloody waste of time, but I suppose it gives them a chance to fill their lungs with good northern fog."

Maisy came in from the back snug and pointed at Sugar.

"Your office is after you, pal."

Sugar got up and answered the phone, spoke, and then looked over and mouthed, "See you later."

Maisy said, "Maggie is in the snug waiting for her pimp, but he won't come in yet as the gaffer is still here. The gaffer is particular about who he pulls a pint for. So the pimp will hang about outside the Grapes, just thought you might like to know?"

I blew her a kiss, got up, and looked up the street. The pimp and his two mates were standing outside the Grapes talking.

"Is Maggie about?"

The three of them looked at me, and out came the blackjacks. I was in no mood for charity. I broke a wrist, caved in a few ribs, and gave the three of them an old-fashioned working over. Lumps would be proud of me. The screams were music to the ears

"Same time next week, lads?"

It had been a hell of a week. Time for some needed peace: a bit of classic jazz and a Rémy. As I put the key in the door, somebody slapped my rear end. I whirled around to see Jackie.

"Don't you just love a man with muscular buttocks? Kimiko said you needed some TLC."

Eneko Sora Detective Series

There are eight books in the Eneko Sora Detective series.
The books are all based in the early 1950s—a time of
stress, crime and poverty following on from the end of
WW11. The city is Liverpool, the gateway to North
America, and all the liners that used the great port to
move cargo from around the world. The world has
moved on from WW11, a new breed of criminal has
arrived—brutal and only interested in money. They need
to be addressed and Eneko and friends are heading the
fight. Nothing is what it seems in this ever-changing city.

The books are:

1 The Missing Samurai Sword
2 The Malacca Umbrella
3 The Spanish Connection
4 The Red Scarf Killer
5 The Forgotten Children
6 Shadows In The Mirror
8 The Tunnels
8 The Final Kill

The Ebook will be on sale shortly and the rest of the
series will appear in print and in Ebook form over the
coming 12 months.

For more information and how to preorder, check the
website: www. yamapublishing.com

I'd be delighted to receive feedback on the books, email:
enekosora@gmail.com

Acknowledgements

This would have been a duller book if not for my editor—my daughter Jennie, and the cover design by Stephen Hearst. I am also grateful to friends for, first, taking the time to read the book and for their constructive feedback. And also to my brother for his encouragement when it seemed to be a hard, never-ending slog. As one friend, Angus, said it will change your life.

Any mistakes or errors in this book are are mine

David Scurlock